DAISY

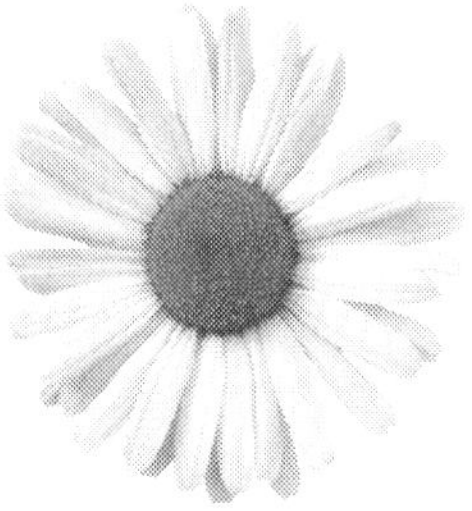

"The life you are born into is an accident of birth."

"How you live that life is what really matters."

PAT BACKLEY

DAISY

Pat Backley
www.patbackley.com

Paperback: ISBN: 978-0-473-54038-8
ebook: ISBN: 978-0-473-54039-5

Edited by Colleen Ward.

Cover design by 100 Covers.com
Formatting by Formattedbooks.com

CONTENTS

ACKNOWLEDGMENTS

I would like to thank everybody who has inspired me to write this book, especially my beloved daughter, Lucy.

Sometimes, people come into your life for no apparent reason, but they end up leaving their footprints on your soul.

There have been many people who have influenced me in some way (far too many to mention by name) and they know who they are.

Thank you.

PROLOGUE
LONDON
1974

They sat on the damp grass making daisy chains.

One large white hand and one small black one, clutching the pretty little flowers.

"Mum, why am I called Daisy?"

CUMMINGS PLANTATION
ALABAMA
1887

Theobold Cummings was born in 1887, into a life of luxury.

His family had owned their cotton plantation in Alabama for more than a century, each generation passing it down to the next.

At one time, they owned almost one hundred slaves, but now all the workers were free men and women.

Though born into this world of riches, Baby Theobold had three older brothers,so he would never inherit any of his family's success.

He would have to make his mark on the world in another way.

EAST END OF LONDON
1887

Illegitimate.

Unwanted.

Polly sobbed quietly as she looked down at the baby in her arms.

She couldn't bear the thought that anyone would call her beautiful little girl such names.

But it was true.

Her little Daisy was a bastard child.

"Now, now girl, stop that whining. You got yourself into this mess, so it's no good crying over spilled milk."

The old woman spoke kindly, but firmly.

She had seen so many young girls in the same predicament and could offer no real words of comfort. She knew exactly how hard their lives would be, now that they had a baby.

And no husband.

For many years, she had acted as an unofficial midwife in the slums of the East End, helping those poor women who could not afford a proper doctor.

She had been called to the house in Stepney by her friend Sybil.

Sybil was a cook at one of the big mansions on the edge of Regents Park, but she always came back to the East End to visit her family on her Sunday afternoons off.

The midwife had been surprised when she got the message.

This family wasn't the kind that gave tea parties and she knew that Sybil only had nephews.

But the boy who delivered the note had said it was urgent.

"I just thought it would be nice to give her an outing," sobbed Sybil.

"I never knew her time was so close, otherwise I wouldn't have done it."

"In fact, none of us even knew she was expecting 'til a few weeks ago."

"She hid it very well. Still fit into her uniform and everything."

Polly sat on the bed and tried to pretend it wasn't happening.

That it wasn't her they were talking about.

Just a few months ago her life had seemed perfect.

Well, almost perfect.

If she didn't think about the extra attention.

Polly had been born in the Workhouse.

Her mother had died during childbirth and she never knew if she had any other family.

Polly had lived a grim existence, made grimmer by the fact that she was rather beautiful and had a sunny disposition.

Both of these were qualities that sometimes made other people envious.

She was put to work when she was just six years old, scrubbing the hard concrete floors of the Workhouse. After a couple of years, she had hands like those of an old woman, red and constantly sore. She hated them.

One day, instead of being on the floor, scrubbing endlessly, she was sent to work in the Laundry. It was then that her life changed.

A pile of sheets that were old and well-worn needed mending.

In the Workhouse, you learnt things just by watching others. This is how Polly learned to read and write; while the children were supposed to have proper lessons, they were only invited in the schoolroom when rich benefactors were visiting. The rest of the time they were treated like slaves, worked to the bone to earn their bed and board. Because of this, any skills came from observation.

Polly was smart, as well as beautiful, and despite her limited opportunities, she was determined to create a better life for herself. Occasionally, she would sneak books from the schoolroom to read by candlelight after the other girls had gone to sleep. While it took her a long time to be able to read and write, by the age of 10, Polly was able to read simple sentences and write her own name.

In much the same way the children got their "education," Polly knew how to sew from watching others do it in the Workhouse.

The day Polly was sent to the laundry, she realised she had found a way out.

A way out of the Workhouse and poverty.

"Well, obviously not for a few years" she thought aloud.

"I am still only small, but one day I will escape all this and become a lady."

That first day in the laundry, Polly recognized she was good at sewing.

Not just capable like some of the other girls, but good. Really good.

She excelled at creating the tiniest little stitches that were just about invisible to the naked eye.

And best of all, she loved doing it.

"Course, I suppose it's in her blood. Her mother was a wonder with a needle."

Polly was thrilled. She had never heard anyone talk about her mother like that.

"Did you know my mother?" she asked the old woman who had spoken.

"Of course. Everyone knew her."

"She was already expecting you when she came here, great big belly she had, and was half dead with cold and hunger. But very beautiful, like you, and so good with a needle. The master got her doing all the fancy work."

From that day on, Polly was determined to be the best seamstress ever, as good as her mother had been.

And so successful was she, that when she was just eleven years old she was sent out from the Workhouse. To go into service as a junior sewing maid in a big house on Cornwall Terrace, on the southwest corner of Regents Park.

She had been so happy.

In the new house, the other servants had taken the little girl under their wings.

She spent hours in her little room in the basement, next to the kitchen, sewing beautiful dresses for the mistress of the house.

Sybil, the cook, had shown Polly great kindness from the very first day she had arrived at the big house, a skinny and frightened child, straight from the Workhouse.

"I just look at that little mite and think how lucky we all are," Sybil had said to no-one in particular in the servants hall that evening, after all the younger ones had gone to bed.

"Still, at least she's all safely tucked up here now and we can keep an eye on her."

"My old Gran was always terrified of ending up in the Workhouse..." said Mr. Briggs, the butler.

"...and the thought of ending up in a Pauper's Grave haunted her."

They all nodded in agreement.

Every servant in that grand house had started life in poverty.

Getting a job "in service" was considered a real step up in the world.

It meant an escape from the worry and grind of everyday life in the slums.

Their jobs were hard of course, up with the lark and slaving away all day, but although they grumbled, they were grateful enough for their lot.

Wages were poor, but they had free board and lodging. This meant they were able to save a little and help their families survive back home.

As the years passed Polly grew more beautiful, although this went largely unnoticed. She spent every day in her little room next to the kitchen, creating the most exquisite gowns, embellished with frills, lace, and delicate embroidery. Gowns that all her mistress's friends envied.

"Do tell us, my dear Mrs. Fox-Leighton, where on earth you found this wonderful dressmaker. Where is her workshop?"

"Yes, do tell, I want her to make my entire collection for next season."

"Oh my dears, it is a secret really. But I will tell you, just as long as you promise to keep it to yourselves."

Of course she knew that as soon as they left the soirée, it would be all around London. These women were such dreadful gossips.

She cleared her throat, ensuring she had their full attention before she spoke.

"Actually, she comes from Paris. Trained with some of the finest fashion houses there, I believe."

She coloured slightly as she said this. Of course she knew that Polly, as an eleven-year-old orphan, had come from the Workhouse, not from Paris at all.

She had only taken her on because the master of the Workhouse had recommended her good sewing skills. In her wildest dreams she had never imagined that a child from the slums of the East End could create such fine dresses, so fine that she would become the envy of the town. And she had no intention of sharing her with anybody!

"But of course, like so many artistic people, she is rather highly strung and prefers to keep her client list very small and exclusive."

So Polly never got the chance to sew for anyone else. Instead, she spent every waking hour creating beauty for her mistress. Nothing pretty for herself of course; she was only allowed to wear plain, grey, scratchy servant dresses, with her beautiful blonde curls tucked firmly into a white cotton cap.

Nonetheless, she was happy. She shared an attic bedroom with the three young parlour-maids and ate all her meals round the long table with the other servants. For the first time in her life, she felt like part of a family.

The house on Cornwall Terrace was opposite Regents Park, so on their Sunday afternoons off, Polly and the other girls would sometimes take a stroll in the park.

"Hey Poll, do you mind waiting here for us? We won't be long."

Polly nodded and smiled. She knew that both girls had sweethearts and that Sunday afternoons were the only times they could see them.

She was just happy to be out in the fresh air. She loved her little sewing room, but it was in the basement with no window, so it was a luxury to be out in the real world, watching everybody go about their business.

She sat down on the grass and stretched out her legs, taking care not to show too much ankle. The grass was full of daisies and she idly picked some.

"These will look so pretty on my table," she thought to herself.

And then another thought popped into her head.

"Daisy, what a pretty name."

"If I ever have a little girl that's what I'll call her........ Daisy."

..................It was Easter Sunday and Polly was alone in the servants' hall.

All the others had gone to spend the afternoon with their families.

She didn't mind; it was nice to have some peace and quiet, and she was trying to finish a ball gown that the mistress wanted to wear on her return from the country.

The Fox-Leightons were very wealthy and as well as the mansion on Cornwall Terrace, they had a country house in Sussex. The whole family and a few servants had gone there for the Easter holidays.

So Polly was rather surprised to hear the bell ringing from the upstairs sitting room. The bells, one for every room in the house (except the servants' quarters of course) were on a board in the basement corridor, each clearly labelled so they could be responded to immediately.

The bell rang again.

"Must just be the wind," she thought aloud.

When it rang for the fourth time however, she began to get frightened.

"Perhaps there really are ghosts here after all."

Fred, the young footman, would often tease her, creeping into her sewing room when she was still working late at night after all the others had gone to bed. She knew he was only trying to frighten her so that he could carry her candle and escort her safely up to the attic. She also knew that he was just being kind and had no bad intentions, for his interest lay with boys, not girls.

She heard loud footsteps coming down the basement stairs and grabbed her largest pair of scissors. "Not much of a weapon, but it is the best I can do!" she thought.

"Why didn't you answer my bell?"

Her heart stopped pounding. It was just the master, Mr. Fox-Leighton.

She looked up at him. "I'm so sorry sir. I thought you were a ghost."

He laughed.

"Oh God, do I look that ancient?"

Polly was flustered. She had never even spoken to him before. The only time she was allowed upstairs was to fit the mistress for a new gown, and of course that never happened when he was around.

It was a warm afternoon, there was no window in her sewing room and because she had thought she was all alone in the house, she had taken off her cap. Her long blonde curls were falling down to her shoulders.

"What pretty hair you have, why haven't I noticed it before? Remind me what your name is."

Obviously, he had mistaken her for one of the parlour maids, who spent all their days working in the upstairs rooms.

"Um, I'm Polly, sir."

"And why are you all alone down here?"

He spoke loudly, with the air of authority that comes with wealth and power.

"Um, the others have all gone to visit their families, sir, what with it being Easter Sunday..."

"And why, little Polly, are you not gone to see yours?"

She gulped, trying to stifle a cry. "I don't have no-one sir. I'm an orphan."

"Not even any brothers or sisters, or wicked uncles?"

She laughed nervously. "No sir, no one at all."

It happened so quickly.

If she had been older and more experienced, she might have anticipated his intentions and could perhaps have stopped him. But she was only just sixteen and had never even been kissed.

He was a strong, virile man, used to getting his own way, and she was too shocked and terrified to even cry out. Perhaps he took her silence as consent.

And after that, of course he wanted more.

The next time his wife was staying with the children at their country house, he asked the butler to send up "that girl who does the sewing. I have a waistcoat that needs altering and I daresay she hasn't got much to do now my wife is away."

He hardly went to the country anymore.

His wife and family went most weekends, but he stayed behind, using work as an excuse. He worked in his father's bank, one he would inherit someday. The same bank that paid for all his wife's extravagances.

His wife never made a fuss about his absences. Obviously, she had her suspicions. She had had to get rid of two young maids in the last few years. They had both wept and wailed when she sent them packing, with their swelling bellies and no references. She had chosen to ignore her nagging feelings each time regarding how they came to be in that condition whilst living in her home.

In his own selfish way, the master became quite fond of Polly.

Besotted by her youth, beauty, and innocence, he got a perverse thrill out of knowing he was the first man to possess her.

The older servants became anxious. They knew exactly how this would end. Their poor Polly would be thrown out on the street, dumped in the gutter as soon as he tired of her.

Polly tried to pretend it wasn't happening. She was used to the unwanted attention now, and at least he wasn't cruel to her. In fact, sometimes he seemed to genuinely care about her.

But this was different. This was the end.

No-one noticed her swelling body. She just let out the seams of her dresses and made a voluminous white apron to wear over them.

"It's just to stop any dirt from my dress getting onto the fine lace." she explained one day to Sybil.

Polly managed to conceal her pregnancy for months, even from the master.

He was always in such a hurry that most of her clothes stayed on anyway, so he never noticed her bump.

But one evening, as she and the girls were undressing for bed, she forgot to turn her back.

"Oh my lawd Poll, are you up the duff?"

It was the worst thing that could happen to a servant girl and they all knew it. It made no difference that their master had fathered the child, because of course, everyone knew he had. And they all just waited for Polly to be dismissed.

But they were wrong. Mr. Fox-Leighton had grown genuinely fond of Polly, and when he heard that she had given birth to a baby girl, he insisted that Sybil bring them both back to the house after her confinement.

"Where did she have the baby? Are they both well?"

He had wandered down to the kitchen.

Sybil wanted to shout at him, to tell him what a selfish bastard he was to ruin all these young girls' lives. But she couldn't afford to lose her position, so she kept those thoughts to herself.

"Yes sir, they're both doing well and baby Daisy is a dear little thing. Beautiful like her mother. They're staying with my sister in Stepney at present. Polly went into labour when we were visiting there on Sunday."

"Good to hear, bring them back as soon as she can travel; the baby can stay down here in the kitchen with you all."

Sybil was stunned, too stunned to respond. But she had noticed the way his voice softened when he spoke of Polly.

Maybe it was going to be alright after all.

Things were alright for a while.

Daisy was such a good baby and mostly laid quietly in her little wooden cot beside Polly's sewing table. Of course, she was spoilt outrageously by all the other servants.

"It's so good to have a little one around," Sybil said.

"I think it's because she reminds us all of our families back home."

"At least we get to cuddle her whenever we like! Now, we don't just have to wait for Sunday afternoons."

Kitty, one of the parlour-maids, spoke wistfully. She had a sweetheart and was desperate to get married and have babies, but that was just a dream until her Sid earnt enough money to support them both.

"Well, I think she's just the most beautiful baby that ever lived,"

Fred the footman spoke with such passion that they all laughed.

"Oh Fred, you're always so dramatic."

He had turned out to be a very good friend to Polly.

When she first came back to the house after Daisy's birth, she had been terrified that the other servants of the house would judge her and ignore the little baby girl. How wrong she had been.

Truthfully, all of them came from poor homes; most of them had sisters or cousins who had fallen prey to unsuitable men, or just innocent love, and had ended up unmarried with a baby. Society might judge her harshly, but these good people didn't.

Mrs. Fox-Leighton, their mistress, didn't show Polly the same compassion, of course. However, she tolerated the rumours because she wanted to keep her "Parisian-trained dressmaker" at her beck and call.

Often Polly was sewing through the night and into the early hours of the morning, creating lavish gowns with intricate embroidery while her eyes strained to see properly in the candlelight. At times like this, all she really wanted was to be tucked up in her bed in the attic dormitory, with Daisy sleeping safely beside her.

"Oh Poll, why don't you call it a night? You look so tired."

Fred had crept downstairs to check on her.

"I'm okay Fred, the mistress wants this gown done by the morning."

Fred made a noise, something between a grunt and a sigh.

"Oh Poll, I hate the way she works you so hard."

They both knew it was the only way their mistress could get her revenge and Polly needed the job so she could keep a roof over the heads of both herself and Daisy. She would kill anyone who ever tried to hurt her baby, and there was no way she would ever let her grow up in the Workhouse.

"Anyway Poll, let me take the little one into the warm kitchen and give her a cuddle while you're getting on with that."

And that became a pattern. One for which Polly was so grateful.

Fred had a difficult time before he came to the big house on Cornwall Terrace.

As one of twelve children in total (most of whom had died in infancy, as disease was rife in the overcrowded slums), he was the youngest of three boys. His brothers were big, strapping lads, able to hold their own in a street fight, but Fred was smaller and lighter, with an almost girlish physique. He was quiet and gentle by nature, and hated it when his dad called him a pansy boy.

"So, you're going into service, Fred? To be a rich man's tart I suppose?"

Those had been his father's parting words when Fred left home at the tender age of just 13 to work in the big house.

Fred sat in the warm kitchen, nestling baby Daisy in his arms while tears ran down his cheeks. He was only 26 years old, but knew he would never be able to marry and have a little one like this of his own. Those things just weren't possible for someone like him, a man who preferred the company of men, rather than pretty girls.

Daisy grew quickly and was soon toddling around the kitchen, getting into mischief. A few of the older, grumpier servants muttered about the "wrong side of the blanket, don't know why the Missus tolerates her," but Daisy was blissfully unaware of such bitterness. She was a happy and contented little girl, certain of her place in the world.

On her 2nd birthday, there was a little party in the kitchen. Sybil had baked a cake and Polly had made a pretty little dress from leftover scraps of satin and lace.

"Am I interrupting something?"

They all started at the master's voice. He never came downstairs.

Well not since that first day, that Easter morning, when he had treated Polly so badly.

Sybil recovered first.

"Oh yes, sir, we're just having a little party to celebrate our Daisy's 2nd birthday."

She put the emphasis on "our Daisy's" to let him know that, although he wanted nothing to do with his child, there were plenty of other people who loved her.

Polly kept quiet and tried to merge into the background, hoping he wouldn't notice her. She hated his attention. Just a few months after Daisy's birth, he had demanded that she return to his bed. Thank God she had managed to avoid getting pregnant again.

"My word, what a lovely little thing you are."

He had bent down to speak to Daisy. "And how old are you?"

"I'm two."

"It's my birthday."

"Well, I think that means you are big enough now to come up to the nursery and play with my boys."

You could have cut the atmosphere in the kitchen with a knife. He had never even laid eyes on his daughter until today and now he was demanding she go upstairs.

And so it began.

Every morning, as soon as she woke, one of the maids took Daisy up to the nursery for breakfast. She spent all her days up there, ate every meal up there, and became the family pet. The master's sons were nice enough boys, a few years older than Daisy, and she was a novelty to them as they had no sisters. The two nannies had known her since she was a baby, so at least she was still surrounded by love.

But Polly was bereft. The new arrangement meant she only saw her beloved daughter first thing in the morning and when it was time to put her to bed at night. By then, Daisy was too tired to play or even listen to a story. The only time they got to spend together was Sunday afternoons.

If the weather was good, they often spent these afternoons in Regents Park and Daisy demanded they find patches of flowers growing in the grass.

"Mum, will you make me a daisy crown and a bracelet and a necklace?"

Polly laughed. She knew that when they got back to the house and everyone was gathered 'round the big table having a late supper, the little girl wanted to make a grand entrance.

"They will all think I am such a lady in my lovely Daisy jewellery."

Polly treasured these precious moments and would hug the little girl so tightly that she would squeal and complain," Mum, you're squishing my new bonnet."

Daisy was blissfully unaware that there was any difference between her and Thomas or William. She knew that they weren't her real brothers of course. The boys slept upstairs in big bedrooms, with their nannies in the adjoining room, while she went up to the attic to share the little room with her Mum and the three housemaids. But, she had beautiful clothes, made by Polly, from the scraps of the mistress's gowns. When Daisy had first started spending her days upstairs, the mistress sent a message to Polly:

"If I have to tolerate that child in my house, I insist she will at least be decently dressed. Use whatever you need from my cut offs."

Polly suffered in silence. Her precious daughter now spent all her time upstairs, with the sons of the man who had raped her.

And then she realised she was pregnant again.

She was violently sick every morning.

And when she finally went into labour in her little sewing room, surrounded by satin, ribbons, and lace, it all went horribly wrong. She died in agony, her unborn baby still inside her.

Polly died on a Thursday evening.

They were all in shock. Why on earth had their beautiful, loving girl been snatched so cruelly from them. From her little daughter?

Mr. Briggs took control. Although his manner was stern, he was actually a very kind man and he too had adored Polly.

"Oh, it's so unfair." sobbed Kitty.

"Why couldn't it have been that witch upstairs who died, instead of our Poll?"

"She was only 19, had the rest of her life to look forward to."

Mr. Briggs could see that everyone was too distraught to think properly.

"Right," he said.

"I think the best thing we can do for Polly now is tidy things up and get her ready."

The sobs got louder.

"You mean we've got to clean her up and dress her ready to be buried?"

Kitty was beginning to sound hysterical.

"Yes, Mr. Briggs. I think that's the best thing we can do for our girl now."

Sybil's voice quavered as she spoke. Polly had been like a daughter to her.

"Come on Kitty, you can help me."

The two women went into the sewing room and closed the door.

Fred had volunteered to look after Daisy. The little girl had no real idea what was going on; she was not quite three years old and was very distressed.

"When can I see my mum, Fred?"

"Has the baby arrived?"

Fred had to swallow hard and brush away a few tears before he could answer.

"Daisy my darling, I'm so sorry, but you can't see Mum."

"She has gone to Heaven to be with the angels."

"When will she be back?"

Fred couldn't control his tears. He just held the little girl very tightly and stroked her beautiful blonde curls.

"Just like her mum's hair." he thought.

"Thank God she didn't inherit too much from that bastard of a father."

If he had been a bigger man, stronger and less gentle, more like his brothers, Fred would have marched upstairs right then and knocked his master to the ground with no thought of his position. But he was a gentle soul, and although his heart was breaking, he stayed where he was. Comforting her beloved daughter was the best thing he could do for his Poll right now.

Sybil and Kitty worked quietly, both overcome with grief.

First they had to move aside all the fabric, ribbons, and lace that littered the table. The kitchen maids brought them buckets of hot soapy water to clean the floor. Polly had not died in a tidy or dignified way.

Once the room was more organised, they gently lifted her body onto the table and began to prepare her.

Kitty was sobbing loudly.

"Please, please Sybil, let's make her look as beautiful as we can. As beautiful as she was before that monster upstairs killed her."

Sybil just nodded her head in agreement. Normally she would have chided Kitty for being so dramatic, but it was true. Their Polly was dead because of that man.

By the time they were finished, she was in her best Sunday dress. Her golden curls were clean and shiny, and clutched in her hand was a small posy of daisies and rosemary.

None of them could afford to pay for a proper funeral.

"I'm going to see my brother, he works down Finchley cemetery."

Fred spoke quietly.

He made the necessary arrangements and the very next day the four of them (Fred, Sybil, Kitty, and little Daisy) set off for the cemetery on the back of an old horse-drawn wagon.

"I just hate it that she hasn't got a proper coffin."

"At least she has us."

"I wish the little one didn't have to see this though."

"But we couldn't leave her behind, she's upset enough as it is. And the others all have to work, I was surprised Mr. Briggs even gave us the morning off."

"Do you think the mistress will be angry we've gone out?"

"I don't think she'll care; she'll just be glad that she's rid of her rival."

The others cast a warning glance at Kitty, and Sybil squeezed little Daisy's hand.

The poor child looked so sad. Not really understanding anything except that her mum was missing and she had been made to wear this big, scratchy black ribbon on her sleeve. Still, at least she wasn't the only one, the others all had black ribbons on their coats too.

After a while they arrived at the cemetery.

It was a vast and forbidding place on this foggy and chilly winter morning.

"Come on you lot, hurry up. My boss said we're only allowed ten minutes and we have to be done by the time the first proper funeral cortege arrives."

Fred's brother spoke roughly, but only because he was upset to see this motley little crew, come to bury their loved one in such a shabby way.

Most of the funerals he dug the graves for were big, showy affairs, with shiny black carriages and horses with plumes, and lots of wealthy well-dressed mourners.

And the little one. Fred had told him everything last night and he had been so angry that he wanted to go straight over there and kill that damn Mr. Fox-bloody-Leighton. But Fred had stopped him.

"I know, I know, Joe, but we can't help the lass now. The best we can do is see she gets a proper burial."

But of course, it wasn't a proper burial.

Joe had been allowed to dig a grave on the far side of the cemetery, well away from all the posh memorial stones and marble angels.

It was known as the Pauper's Graveyard. It looked just like an ordinary field, with no markings at all to show where the dead lay.

Sybil, Kitty, and Daisy stood by the open grave while Fred and the wagon driver carefully lifted their precious cargo and carried it to the graveside. There was no coffin, none of them had been able to afford one. Their dear Poll was just wrapped tightly in layers of rough fabric, rather like an Egyptian mummy.

"Why are you putting my mum in that horrible hole?"

None of them, not even Joe, was able to respond; they were all so choked up with the utter misery of it all.

Fred put his arm round the little girl.

"Your mum wasn't well my darling. Do you remember I told you last night that she has gone to live with the angels?"

"But the angels don't live in a horrible hole in the ground like that!"

She sobbed loudly and tried to wriggle from his grasp.

"I want to go in there with her. If you unwrap her, I can cuddle her and make her better, then we can all go home."

Even big Joe was in tears. He had attended many funerals, standing behind the grave, waiting to fill in the hole after the mourners had departed, but none had touched his heart like this.

Fred was the only one calm enough to speak, so he said a few words, they all recited the Lord's Prayer, and Daisy threw a small posy of flowers on top of her mother.

"Don't worry Mum, we'll come and take you home when you feel better."

So, Polly was buried in a Pauper's Grave. Not even 20 years old, and no tablet or memorial to say she had ever lived.

Just a few days after Polly died, Sybil had asked to see *him* and the mistress.

"I was just wondering sir, whether you wanted Daisy to stay here?"

"If not, my sister Maisy over in Stepney could take her in. She already has a few children, so another won't go amiss."

"Good, good, best place for her. She will be happier there."

The man who had destroyed Polly's life already had his eye on another housemaid: a pretty young girl who had just come over from Ireland.

She could sense relief from both the Fox-Leightons regarding the departure of little Daisy.

Their only regret was that he had lost his beautiful young conquest and she had lost her gifted seamstress.

At that moment, Sybil couldn't have hated them more.

And so that was that.

The end of Daisy's life in the big house.

CUMMINGS COTTON PLANTATION ALABAMA. DECEMBER 24TH, 1918

The carriages were lined up outside the beautiful, old, white plantation house.

Inside there was a string quartet playing and the sound of excited chattering.

The guests were all rich, beautifully dressed, White folk.

Black servants, in smart white uniforms, wafted round, dispensing drinks and platters of food.

There was an enormous Christmas tree in the corner of the room, beautifully but simply decorated with hundreds of plain white shiny baubles.

To represent the cotton grown on the plantation, hundreds and hundreds of fluffy white cotton balls.

"Attention please."

Jack Theobold Cummings, a tall, once handsome, but now rather time-ravaged man, stood in the centre of the room tapping a silver spoon on his crystal wine glass to attract everyone's attention.

"Welcome folks."

"As y'all know, this little party is not just our regular Christmas Eve party.

This year, we must also celebrate the end of the war to end all wars, and offer our grateful thanks for the safe homecoming of our boys.

He glanced around the room, his eyes resting for a few seconds on two couples.

"And of course, we have to remember the ultimate sacrifice made by those who didn't make it home. We will grieve them forever."

He paused dramatically, giving the assembled audience time to reflect.

"Now, y'all may think this is not the appropriate time, but I am proud to say I have another important announcement to make."

The silence was palpable.

"We are also here to celebrate."

"My wife and I are delighted to announce the engagement of our youngest boy, Theobold, to the lovely Melissa Cobb."

"Come here boy. You too, Melissa. Let our guests see what a fine couple you make."

Theobald (more usually known as Theo) had always been a bit of an enigma. Even as a little boy.

He wasn't like his three elder brothers.

They all loved being part of the plantation, well, they loved the lifestyle it afforded them. They didn't actually do any real work, but were all very good at marching round and giving orders to all.

Theo's brothers were much older than him, so by the time he turned twelve, they were all married with fine establishments of their own. They had all married well of course, two had wives who were daughters of other big plantation owners and the third had found himself a rich heiress, an Earl's daughter no less, when he did the Grand Tour in Europe. She was used to fine living and servants and adapted very well to her new life in Alabama, despite her constant complaints about the searing summer heat.

"She sits under her parasol on the shady porch, sipping lemonade and looking over the fields. The same fields where our people are slaving out there day after day in the blazing sun, picking cotton so that she can have a life of luxury! And they never complain."

Theo spoke with such passion. Since he was a little boy, he had been aware of the differences in the way his family lived compared to all their workers.

His best friends were children of the cotton pickers.

Like him, they had all been born into plantation life. Some of them were descended from the original family slaves who had chosen to stay on the plantation as free men and women after Abolition.

In Theo's view, they were still treated as little better than slaves by his father and brothers.

"But why, just because someone has black skin, should they be treated differently?"

"What gives us the right to think we are superior, just because we are White?"

His father would get so angry when he spoke like that.

"We have to do somethin' about that boy," he said to his wife one evening as they were getting ready for bed.

Pearl was brushing her mistress's hair, but of course with her black skin, she was quite invisible to them both.

"Oh Jack, don't fret so. Once he settles down with a nice wife and starts behaving like a proper Southern gentleman, he will forget all these silly notions about servants being our equals."

Pearl winced. She had worked for the mistress for 25 years, since she was 10 years old. Chosen for her quiet manner and obedience. But inside, she was a seething mass of resentment.

She lived with her parents, grandmother, three sisters, and their families, in the old slave quarters in the garden. Close enough to be at their master's beck and call, but far enough away that the rich family and their rich friends didn't have to look at them.

"That boy just needs to learn to keep his mouth shut. Those thoughts will get him into trouble one day. Did you see the way old Jefferies looked at him when he was going on about Blacks being equal?"

It was a well-known secret that old man Jefferies and several others of their acquaintance were still active members of the Ku Klux Klan. Although official records said that the Klan was disbanded back in 1870, everyone in Alabama knew the truth.

Theo's father was not a particularly bad man; he just came from a long line of privileged white plantation owners. The life he led was the only one he knew. Black people had always worked in his family's cotton fields.

He could still remember being eight years old in 1865 and learning that the Civil War had come to an end. His father (Theo's grandfather) had been extremely distraught.

"After all that bloody sacrifice!"

He had never heard his father roar like that.

General Robert Lee had just surrendered. The Confederate Party had collapsed after four years of intense combat, and the South had suffered a huge cost to human life, both White and Black. The Southern States were in chaos, and slavery was finally abolished.

Most of the slaves on the Cummings plantation, now free men and women, had chosen to stay in the fields. They knew no other life, and their master had not been as cruel as some others they had heard of.

As she continued to brush her mistress's hair, Pearl thought about her grandmother, Bess. Bess was a tiny, wizened old lady. Bent double after decades of picking cotton, but with a mind as sharp as a tack. She wondered what she would make of this conversation when she relayed it later.

"Girl, stop your complaining. At least you don't get beaten every week or worry that your boy is going to get himself lynched. Or that the master is going to take a fancy to you and you'll end up with a whole bunch of mulatto babies."

Bess spoke with a catch in her voice. Even after all these years, it still haunted her that she and other slaves on the plantation had been forcibly impregnated by their owner. And that those babies had then become his *property*, to do with as he chose.

"You think you have a bad life now my girl, but let me tell you. It's paradise to what we had before."

"All of us, men, women, and children, had to work long hours in the hot sun, bent over pretty much double, picking that cotton. Then carrying it in baskets on our heads, for the overseer to check. If he didn't like what we got, he would whip us. Sometimes we had to stop picking to feed our babies. We used to put them in their baskets, keep 'em right there in the fields with us. But the master let us stop to feed them when they needed it, 'cos we were making more new slaves for him."

She stopped for a moment, overcome with emotion.

"But we taught all our children, even those babies, how to find the North Star, that way they might be able to find their way to freedom.

And we taught them songs, especially the ones that our old people had taught us."

Her sweet old voice filled the air.... "I look'd over Jordan and what did I see? Coming for to carry me home."

Pearl rushed over to the old lady and hugged her. Then she went to get Old Freddie. He was the only one who could calm Bess down when she got upset like this.

Bess and Old Freddie were the only original slaves left on the property. The others had all died long before their time, of overwork or disease.

Every afternoon, at exactly two o'clock, the ancient old pair would sit on the wooden bench under the old oak tree and talk. They always had so much to talk about, so many memories. So many shared sorrows.

ALABAMA
1908

When Theo was 21 years old, his father decided to send him away.

"That boy needs to change his ways. He spends far too much time with the servants, doesn't concentrate on his studies, and has no interest in girls."

They had tried to match-make, introducing him to all the suitable young women within a 50-mile radius of the plantation. There had been balls and parties, picnics and outings, and although Theo had behaved in his usual impeccable, well-mannered Southern way, he had made it quite obvious that none of these pretty, vacuous young ladies were right for him.

"Any young gal with half a mind would be delighted to have him, even though he doesn't have much to recommend himself personality wise. He comes from a good family and will get a good marriage settlement."

For once, Jack's wife stood up to him. She loved her youngest son dearly.

"Oh darling, I do think you're being a bit harsh. Theo just hasn't found the right girl yet. Perhaps he will be like Robert and choose a nice heiress. I agree that we should let him go travelling; Europe will broaden his mind."

"Actually, I was thinking I might send him to England too. He could visit some of the mills where we send our cotton."

And so it was decided. Theo set off in February 1909, at the age of just 22, for his big adventure.

THE WORLD
1909

Of course, Theo hadn't been allowed to travel alone. His manservant, Matty, accompanied him, and what adventures they had!

They had been friends since they were children. Matty was the grandson of Old Freddie and lived on the plantation. He had been given the job as Theo's manservant when the boys were just eleven years old.

"They spend all their time together, so we might as well give the boy a job and a title."

Theo's father had said this when his other sons complained that they weren't given their own servants until they were 18.

The two young boys had a wonderful time growing up together.

Matty was only a few months older than Theo, and of course was never treated as anything less than a brother by the younger boy.

So, as they travelled through Europe for their "Grand Tour," these two tall and very handsome young men attracted a lot of attention. They never gave any thought to their different skin colours, so it came as a surprise when people found them "an exotic pair."

They were invited to parties and balls wherever they went.

At the Carnivale in Venice, they lost their tour guide in the foggy February alleyways, and emerged to find themselves outside a palace on the Grand Canal, each wrapped in the arms of a courtesan. They smoked hookah pipes in Morocco, waltzed in Vienna, gambled on the Cote D'Azur, and rode camels in the Sahara. In short, they had an absolutely wonderful time and the plantation in Alabama seemed like another world.

After the boys spent four years aimlessly wandering around with no rich heiresses in sight, Theo's father began to make demands. He sent telegraphs, threatening to cut off Theo's allowance unless he found a wife.

Theo replied.

"Dear Father, thank you for your concern. I have searched high and low, throughout Europe and beyond, for a woman suitable to bring home to you, but to no avail. I was thinking that perhaps we should now go to England as you wanted, to visit the cotton mills of Lancashire. Perhaps there, I will find a nice English bride."

And so they travelled to England. These two handsome and by now, quite worldly and experienced young men, were still as close, if not closer, than brothers could be.

First, they went to London for a few weeks to stay with an elderly relative. Theo's great uncle, Walter, had left Alabama to see the world and never returned. Years later, he was now thrilled to have the company of Theo and Matty.

Walter lived in a large house in Cornwall Terrace on the edge of Regents Park.

The travelling pair thought that Cornwall Terrace was a splendid example of terraced mansions in the Greco-Roman style, which were designed by John Nash.

By now, both Theo and Matty had acquired a great love of architecture.

They had seen many of Europe's finest buildings and had marvelled at some of the World's Wonders, like the Great Pyramid of Giza and the story of the Colossus of Rhodes. They had crossed the Alps, where Hannibal had marched through with his army of elephants. They spent weeks in Rome, imagining themselves as Roman soldiers at the Colosseum and the Pantheon, and they had flirted outrageously with all the beautiful Italian girls.

But now, it was time for some serious thinking.

Theo had promised his father that he would visit some of the mills, where their cotton was sent to be turned into fabric. He was dreading it, for it would just remind him that very soon they would be obliged to return home.

Worst of all, he would have to face the reality that Alabama would seem so dull after all he had seen.

"Oh my dear boys, you will just hate the North of England."

"Only been there once myself many years ago, and couldn't wait to get back to London."

"Still, once you've done that boring business, we can have some splendid times here in London before you sail away."

So, on a bright sunny day in 1913, they set off from Euston Station and caught a train to Blackburn in Lancashire.

It wasn't sunny in Blackburn.

In fact, it was very grey. Dull and depressing.

The young men saw some fine mill buildings, mostly red brick, some built of local stone. They were all well-designed, but with a grey sadness about them.

The interior of the mills were even worse.

They were driven on a tour of the surrounding countryside and shown around several large mills.

"And this is India Mill, a fine example of modern machinery, with 84,000 spindles."

"Here at Queen Street Mill, we have over a thousand looms."

"Victoria Mill, 19,000 spindles, Finsley Mill, 48,000 spindles and 1,500 looms."

"Trafalgar Mill, 26,000 spindles and 625 looms."

"Of course since 1906, we have used electricity to drive the machinery, so it's not as noisy as it used to be."

"Maybe not," thought Theo, "but it is still a dreadful place to work."

The noise was horrendous and the weaving looms caused a lot of vibration.

He looked at the raw cotton bales, having just arrived from America, and thought of the fields back home. Endless fields of fluffy, white cotton. But at least there was fresh air for the workers there, not like in these suffocating hell holes.

He asked about the working conditions and learnt that the mills employed many women and children. While they used to have children doing mill work at as early as seven years of age, they now did not employ any children under 12.

"But of course, they don't make old bones. Hands and fingers often get severed, and the dust inhaled gives workers "brown lung." Or they go deaf, or get skin or eye infections, bronchitis, or tuberculosis."

By the time Theo and Matty got to Manchester the next day to visit the trading floor of the Cotton Exchange, they were desperate to leave this dark and depressing part of England. The Exchange was a splendid building of course, but neither of them could forget the dull, sad eyes of the mill workers.

They were both quiet on the return journey to London.

"Now I know what William Blake meant when he wrote about dark, satanic mills in his 'Jerusalem' poem." Theo had always admired William Blake; of course, Blake had abhorred slavery too.

Theo and Matty returned to Alabama in 1914, just before the start of the Great War.

They drifted back into their old life as we all do eventually, even if it was not the life they really wanted to live.

Their son not having brought an heiress home, Theo's parents were even more desperate to find him a suitable bride.

"Oh lord, Matty, on Saturday I have to go to another ball, this time in Montgomery.

Last month they had me in Birmingham; I wouldn't be surprised if they try Tuscaloosa next! When will they realise I don't want one of these pretty, vapid girls they keep serving up?"

Matty and his grandfather shared a smile. How many times had they heard Theo rant like this?

"All I want is a nice, intelligent woman who has the same views as me. She doesn't even have to be young and beautiful. I just need someone who is interested in the world. Someone to have a decent conversation with, who might even want to leave her gilded cage and travel out of the state!"

Old Freddie laughed out loud.

"Master Theo," (as these had been the words he had always used, he could never bring himself to use just the boy's first name)

"I think maybe your list is right, except for the ugly old woman bit."

"We all know you like a pretty face."

Matty laid down the chess piece he was holding.

They had been playing, as they did most evenings, with the Isle of Lewis chess set that Theo had bought in London. They kept it in Old Freddie's cabin, as it was the only place they could be sure of having a quiet game. The big house was always full of people, some of whom didn't approve of Matty being in the house for a social occasion. They much preferred it when he was made to don a smart white uniform and serve drinks to their guests.

Somehow, they seemed to have forgotten that he had been Theo's trusted companion for the whole five years they had been away. Now, back on the plantation, he was just another servant.

It infuriated Theo. How dare they treat his best friend in that despicable way? Matty was more of a brother to him than those puffed up men who bore his same name.

"I just wish you could come to these things with me Matty. They wouldn't be so dreary if you were there. At least we could have a bit of fun."

Matty did go of course, as a carriage driver or manservant, but he was never allowed to enter the ballrooms. He was always sent straight to the kitchen.

The two had been back in Alabama for nearly four years now, and dozens of suitable brides had been selected by his parents just to be completely refused by Theo.

He was an incredibly attractive man. With his tanned skin, white teeth, and fine physique, in addition to his intelligence, compassion, and good manners, he was a fine catch.

"I don't think there's a girl anywhere that you could desire. Leastways not one that your daddy would approve of!" Old Freddie chuckled.

Both young men burst into laughter. They knew exactly how many women Theo had managed to find attractive on their travels. But then, he was just looking for fun. Now he was supposed to be looking for someone to share the rest of his life with.

At the ball in Montgomery, he spotted her.

She was standing alone, watching the dancers. He hated seeing anyone left out, so he wandered over.

"Good evening. My name is Theobold Cummings."

"Oh, hello. I'm Melissa. Don't you just hate all this?"

He was puzzled.

"All this nonsense, I mean. New ball gowns every week, fancy hairstyles and ribbons, all just to snare a husband."

Theo was stunned. He had never, *ever* met a girl like this in Alabama before.

One who obviously didn't care for all the trappings of wealth.

"Would you like to dance?"

"No thanks. Shall we just go sit down and have a chat?"

"Have you read *Uncle Tom's Cabin*?"

She sounded almost accusing.

"Yes, I have."

"And do you know about Harriet Tubman?"

Harriet Tubman had escaped from slavery in 1849.

"I looked at my hands to see if I was the same person now I was free."

"There was such a glory over everything, the sun came like gold through the trees and over the fields and I felt like I was in heaven."

Theo quoted the words he had read so many times.

He looked up to see that the girl had tears in her eyes.

"Do you live on a plantation? Is your daddy kind to his workers?"

Theo paused for a moment before he spoke.

"Well, *he* thinks he is good to them, but I disagree."

"For example, my very best friend, Matty, is not allowed to come to these things with me just because he is Black."

"Apparently he was good enough to be my companion for five years travelling the world, but here in Alabama he is not good enough to be seen in polite society."

She heard the anger in his voice and gently touched his arm with her gloved hand.

Such a tiny hand, he thought, fighting an urge to bend down and kiss it.

His mother suddenly appeared.

"Theobold, darling, there you are. We have been looking everywhere for you."

"So many young ladies want you to mark their dance cards."

He groaned quietly. He loved his mother dearly, but would much rather stay here and chat with Melissa.

But he allowed himself to be dragged away.

Every time there was a break in the dancing, he looked over to where she was sitting. She only got up once, to dance with a rather gawky young man.

At the end of the evening he found her.

"Forgive me, I just wanted to say how much I enjoyed talking to you earlier." "Hopefully we will meet again."

She coloured slightly.

He was a very attractive man after all, even though he was rather old.

"Oh, I'm quite sure we will. My parents drag me to all these things hoping I will find a rich husband."

Theo smiled politely.

"And I am very sure you will have no trouble on that account."

He wanted to add, "because you are passionate and interesting, as well as beautiful," but managed to swallow the words.

"Oh, I think I will be difficult to marry off. I'm not one of those silly girls who is only interested in the latest fashions or how big her allowance is."

"They've been trying to get rid of me for a while, but no one seems brave enough to take on the challenge."

Theo was enchanted.

"At the next ball, will you make an exception and dance with me?"

She smiled. "Only if you promise we can continue our chat about the evils of slavery."

He talked about her incessantly to Matty and Old Freddie.

Not to his family of course; he didn't want to break the spell.

And the next week they did dance. Every dance.

Melissa, who hated dancing normally, just loved being in his arms.

They talked while they danced. They talked in the interval. They talked over supper.

He had never enjoyed talking to someone so much.

Eventually, he confessed his feelings to his parents.

"I think I have found the girl I want to marry."

"Oh my dear boy, that is splendid news! Who have you decided on?"

"Miss Melissa Cobb from Tuskegee."

"Tuskegee, in Macon County? "

"There are some fine houses there. Do they have a plantation?"

Theo bit his tongue.

Here he was, confessing his love and all his parents were interested in was whether her family had money.

"Yes, the house is very elegant. Greek Revival, Antebellum style."

"Built just before the Civil War, I understand."

"Melissa's father was kind enough to tell me the history."

"So, you've met her parents? Have you proposed to the girl already then?"

"No, of course not Father, I thought to talk to you and Mother first, to get your blessing."

Actually, that wasn't strictly true.

He and Melissa already had an understanding.

He had only known her six months, but there was absolutely no doubt in his mind.

Or hers.

And so it was agreed. They would announce their engagement at the plantation's Christmas Eve party.

EAST END OF LONDON
1900

Ten years had passed since Daisy had arrived at the house in Stepney.

She had only been three years old when Sybil dropped her off there one cold and rainy winter morning, just a few weeks after her mother had died.

But the little room she had been given had been warm, both because of the heat coming from the open coal fire and the welcome she received from the family of the house.

"Come on, my little love."

"Sit by the fire and I'll fetch you some hot soup."

Maisy was Sybil's older sister.

Instead of going into service, she had married her sweetheart, John.

John came from the East End too, like his wife.

All his family going back many generations had worked on the River Thames, either as dockers or boatmen.

John was a huge man with a squashed nose from too many street fights after Friday nights at the Rose and Crown. But he was a good husband who worked hard and loved his wife and children with every fibre of his being.

He and Maisy were parents to five strapping boys. There had been a sixth, their eldest, Samuel. Sadly, he had been killed two years ago, just a lad of 15, when he had slipped and was crushed by a pile of heavy containers.

He had only been working at the docks for a few weeks when it happened.

Neither of Samuel's parents had ever really gotten over his death. John was haunted by the memory of that dreadful day every time he went to work.

"John, John, come quick! Your lad's had an accident."

He would never forget the sight of his much loved, first-born son, lying buried beneath a mountain of crates. Both his legs were broken and there was blood all over his face. He lived just long enough to whisper to his father,

"I'm sorry Dad, I've let you down."

If it hadn't been for the other boys and his beloved Maisy, he thought he might have thrown himself in the Thames, ending it all.

But he couldn't. The rest of his family needed him.

The family's house, in the slums of Stepney, was a three-storey tenement.

Maisy, John and the boys inhabited the front half of the ground floor, which consisted of a large kitchen and two small bedrooms. Being on the ground floor meant they had easy access to the little cobbled yard at the back, where there was a shared toilet and a tap for washing. There was often a big queue for both these facilities, as they were shared between all six families living in the house.

But John and Maisy knew how lucky they were. Some of their neighbours had to share one toilet and one tap between 15 or 16 families.

Although the neighbourhood was very poor, it had a great community spirit. Everyone knew what a struggle life was, so they all took great pride in helping each other.

After Samuel died, his parents had both been in the depths of despair.

Yet, they found themselves overcome with kindness.

Meals were delivered to their door, their young sons were watched over by bigger children and a whip-round was held, door to door, to raise enough money to give the boy a decent funeral. It was all a great comfort, at a time when they needed it most.

Maisy and John had lost Samuel the year after Daisy was born.

Daisy had been born in their very house on that Sunday afternoon three years ago, when Sybil had brought Polly to visit them.

Maisy shuddered, remembering the awful day.

"And now we have that poor little orphan girl back again," she whispered to John.

"Maybe looking after her will heal the pain in our hearts."

John nodded in agreement.

They had always loved Daisy. Sybil and Polly had often brought the little girl to visit them.

"At least she's not had to go to strangers."

"Nor back to the workhouse where her poor mum came from."

And so Daisy became part of their large, often chaotic, but very loving family.

She didn't remember much about her mum, but she did remember the daisy chains. After showing them off to everyone in the servant's hall, she used to put them under her pillow when she went to bed. She could still remember how sad she had been when the little flowers were gone, having turned brown and crumbled away.

And then one day, her mum was gone too.

Daisy loved Maisy. She had always loved Maisy.

Maisy was big and soft, and she was always willing to cuddle Daisy and wipe away her tears.

Maisy had not had a formal education. She went for a while to the Ragged School, but then had to stay at home to help her mother with the other children. There were eleven in total, six boys and five girls, and Maisy was the eldest, so it fell on her to be the one who gave up her schooling. However, she was allowed a couple hours off every week to attend Sunday School.

She couldn't read properly, so just looked at all the pictures in the Bible and listened avidly as the teacher recited the book's stories.

"One day, when I'm grown up, I'm going to call my children those lovely names."

And so she did.

As well as Samuel, Maisy and her husband had little John, Matthew, Mark, Luke and Peter.

She had never seemed to manage to have a girl.

But now she had Daisy, and she was determined to give this little girl the best life possible.

Daisy loved Big John too of course, and although he looked scary and she sometimes heard him bawling at the boys, he never once raised his voice, or his fist, to her. The boys all made a fuss of her and Sybil and Fred came to visit most Sundays, so she was a happy and contented little girl.

She didn't even notice how grim Stepney was. To her, it was home.

The dark and cobbled alleyways lit by gas lamps, the hungry, ragged children begging in the street, the London Fog. She just accepted her surroundings as normal.

Daisy loved going for walks with Maisy and Little John. They would go to Whitechapel and Spitalfields, Brick Lane and Hackney, sometimes walking for hours, until it was time for the others to come home from work.

She learnt to watch where she walked when crossing the road, so she didn't step into any of the big piles of mess the horses had left behind.

She only noticed the good things.

She smiled at all the babies in their large prams, parked in the street to get some fresh air. She smiled at the old ladies scrubbing their front steps while gossiping to their neighbours. She smiled at the men standing outside the public houses, nursing their pints of stout or mild ale. She smiled at the scruffy old men queuing outside the East End Doss House. She peered through the doors of the Salvation Army shelter on Hanbury Street in Whitechapel, hoping to get a glimpse of the "coffin beds" her foster brothers had described in such detail. She smiled at the tattered urchins on the street corners selling newspapers. She smiled at the old lady roasting chestnuts and begged Maisy to buy some for the family.

Daisy helped with all the household chores. She did all the family washing outside in the yard using an old tin bucket and a washboard.

She learnt how to cook and clean and sew. Nothing fancy, just mending torn sheets or darning the boys' socks. She looked forward to the weekly visits with Sybil and Fred.

She was happy.

But just after her 13th birthday, it all changed.

She had noticed Maisy's swelling body and knew a baby was on the way.

It was impossible to live in the East End and be unaware of such things; many families had more babies every year, so pregnant women were a constant sight. Most of these babies were born at home, in the slums, with just a local midwife in attendance.

The night Mary was born would stick in Daisy's mind forever.

John had been sent to the pub by the midwife, the very same midwife who had delivered Daisy all those years ago.

"Lord, that girl is a pretty one. Mind you, her mother was a beauty if I remember. And so young. I remember that day very well; a tragic tale."

Daisy didn't realise they were talking about her.

She was too busy trying not to listen to the agonising screams that came from Maisy every time she had a contraction.

"Why is Mum yelling like that?"

Young John was visibly upset. He was 17 now, working on the docks and had a girlfriend. Normally he would have been out with her tonight, but Daisy had begged him to stay at home.

"Why did Dad go to the pub? He should be here to look after Mum."

Daisy was only 13, but she knew exactly why the midwife had sent his father away. John had spent all afternoon pacing the kitchen floor; every time Maisy cried out, he went barging into the bedroom.

"For God's sake woman, can't you do something to help her?"

Even Daisy knew that babies couldn't be hurried.

Eventually, after seven hours of excruciating labour, baby Mary made her way safely into the world. Young John was sent to fetch his father from the pub and by the time he arrived home, a little worse for wear, mother and baby were sitting up in bed looking the picture of health. The midwife had gone, leaving Daisy in charge.

"Oh, my darling girl. Are you alright? I was so worried about you. It seemed so much worse this time, worse than when you had the boys."

"And it's a girl. Daisy my darling, you have a little sister, how wonderful is that?"

Big John bent over the bed and kissed his wife gently on the forehead. He stroked the baby's hand carefully, as if she were made of the most precious and delicate porcelain.

Daisy was so happy. She looked at the baby and whispered quietly, "You and I will be friends and sisters forever. We will have so much fun."

Baby Mary was just six months old when she contracted diphtheria.

Disease was commonplace in the slums, and at first they thought her cough was just croup. But a few days later, she developed a fever and died.

John and Maisy were distraught, having lost a child to tragedy once again.

Daisy was heartbroken too; she had loved that little girl like she was her own.

Somehow they got through the first awful days. Big John cashed in a small insurance policy to pay for her funeral.

"I'm not letting our girl have a pauper's grave" he ranted, half-mad with grief.

The neighbours were wonderful, just as they had been after Samuel. They organised another whip-round and collected enough money to buy some flowers to go on top of the simple coffin. They even arranged to borrow a horse and cart to carry it.

So, on a wet and windy day in 1900, the little neighbourhood of Stepney buried Baby Mary.

The child was laid to rest in Finchley Cemetery, in a plot amongst all the angels and marble memorials.

Mary's grave was just a few steps from where Daisy's mum, Polly, had been laid, exactly ten years before in her pauper's grave.

John went back to work a few days later and the boys were out of the house all day too, so Daisy was the only one who saw Maisy deteriorate.

She stopped caring for the house and insisted that they spent all day every day in front of the fire, talking about her dead baby. This went on for several weeks, which turned into months.

"Why is there never any dinner when we get home?"

"Mum, we work hard all day; we need some decent food to come home to."

"My darling, please let me help you. I'm grieving too."

But Maisy couldn't seem to shake off the blackness that was engulfing her. She tried to block out her pain with gin.

"Mother's Ruin," yelled John. "I won't let you do this to yourself."

Daisy tried desperately to keep it all together.

When the weeping woman eventually nodded off in front of the fire each afternoon Daisy would rush around, cleaning the rooms as best she could and trying to put together a simple meal for the family.

Time went by and Maisy got worse, and the rooms of the house seemed to take on her despair. They assumed that strange smell of poverty — a combination of dirt and hopelessness.

And one day, while Daisy was in the yard trying to scrub the grime from the docks out of the men's shirts, Maisy walked out into the street and threw herself under a passing omnibus.

Sybil had come rushing to the house as soon as she heard about Maisy.

She hated to see the sadness in the family's eyes.

They had all loved her sister so much, and now they would have to live with the guilt forever.

The guilt of thinking that *somehow* they could have saved her, stopped her from taking her own life.

She stayed with them for the first week, helping them through the awful days of the funeral and the aftermath.

Matthew and Mark were both married now and offered to move back in with their wives, to look after their father and Daisy.

"Actually John, I think it would be better if Daisy came to live with me."

"Those girls will be having babies of their own soon and I don't think it will be fair on Daisy; she's been through enough already."

"But I promise I will bring her back every Sunday to see you."

John was too exhausted to argue. He knew Sybil was right, and he knew that his sister-in-law had always loved the girl.

MARYLEBONE, LONDON. 1901

So, in 1901, the same year the old queen died, Daisy left the slums of Stepney.

She was almost 14 years old when she moved to the mansion in Montague Square, in Marylebone.

The house was owned by Mr. Frederick Palmer, and he welcomed Daisy with open arms.

"My dear child, welcome, welcome."

She had never met anyone quite like him before.

Of course she had seen a few toffs around the slums, but they were usually looking for a willing girl or to offer salvation to some poor wretch outside the gin houses.

"I am delighted you have decided to come and reside with us."

"We are quite a jolly household; I think you will find us to your satisfaction."

Sybil and Fred exchanged a grin. How would their Daisy react to this?

"I'm sure I shall, sir. Thank you for letting me stay."

The house was magnificent. Everything about it was grand, from the huge, shiny black front door with a lion's head knocker, to the enormous black and white tiled hallway. There were six reception rooms, eight bedrooms, four bathrooms, and a mews house in the cobbled yard.

Frederick Palmer was a gentleman in every sense of the word.

Charming and well-mannered, considerate, kind, and generous.

Still handsome, even in his 50th year.

He had never been married nor fathered children. He preferred the company of men, which was totally unacceptable to most members of polite society. He had always been discreet in his liaisons, and so now, in what some considered his dotage, he was viewed merely as rather eccentric.

He had met young Fred when he called at the house on Cornwall Terrace to visit his banker, Mr. Fox-Leighton.

He had noticed the attractive young footman at once and sensed a kindred spirit.

As he was leaving, he slipped a calling card into Fred's hand.

Fred had kept the card in his pocket for an entire year.

From time to time, he took it out and ran his fingers over the embossed gold lettering. Doing anything with the card felt like stepping into another world, a world he longed to step into, but was much too afraid.

On the day his mistress sent away yet another weeping housemaid, her belly swollen with the master's child, he snapped. The girl reminded him of Polly and he felt his heart breaking all over again. He had truly loved her, not in a sexual way, but with deep and real affection.

He wrote out his letter of resignation and left the next day, not caring that he would never get a reference.

And shortly after, he called on Mr. Palmer.

He had been working in the mansion on Montague Square for seven years now, and they had been the happiest years of his life.

It was a strictly business arrangement.

Fred was the head butler and had his own living quarters in the basement, next to the kitchen.

But in the evenings, he and Frederick would sit together in the library, talking and drinking whisky.

They were never lovers, but quickly became best friends.

An unlikely alliance: a boy from the slums and a rich, aristocratic gentleman.

Fred had finally persuaded Sybil to leave Cornwall Terrace and join him on Montague Square.

"Oh Fred, I don't know. Supposing I don't like it. I'm not used to that sort of thing."

"Don't be ridiculous, Sybil. Would you really rather spend your life working for a bastard who gets all his young maids pregnant, then dumps them?"

So, Sybil resigned from the Fox-Leighton household and became the head cook for Mr. Palmer, where she had been for five years now. Frederick had insisted on taking on three young kitchen maids to help her, so her life was much easier than ever before. Not to mention she now had entire Sundays off, rather than just the afternoons.

While she had been away in Stepney following Maisy's suicide, Fred had been noticeably upset and quiet.

"My dear boy, is there anything I can do to help?"

Frederick laid his old, wrinkled hand on Fred's arm. Fred stroked it gently.

"Thanks so much for caring, Fred. I don't know what I'd do without your kindness."

In private, he called his master Fred. They both knew without an ounce of doubt that if Frederick had been twenty years younger, their relationship would be very different. Passionate definitely, but probably with no lasting friendship. And they both cherished the friendship they had.

Alone in the library, they could just relax and be themselves. No pretences, no secrets.

"So, really, there must be something I can do. Not much point being one of the richest men in London if I can't help a friend in his time of need."

Young Fred smiled.

"You've already done so much for me."

"Given me a lovely home, promoted me to head butler, taken on Sybil."

"Nonsense my dear boy. You have brought so much joy to my life, and Sybil gives so much joy to my stomach!"

"Well, I'm worried about our Daisy. You know, Polly's daughter."

He had told the older man about Polly's sad story years ago, shortly after his arrival at the mansion.

"It's alright at the moment, Sybil's there sorting everything out, but I'm not sure it's a good place for her to be on her own, now Maisy's gone."

"I don't think it's right, a pretty young girl like that being on her own in a house full of grown men."

"Why don't you bring her here?"

And so it was decided. And Daisy began her life again at the age of 14.

She was a beautiful girl, with long, golden curls, just like her mother.

Frederick had wanted to give her one of the guest bedrooms and treat her like a daughter, but Fred and Sybil intervened.

"Sir, I know you are being very kind and thoughtful, but I think it would be too much."

"Rubbish Sybil, it will be delightful to have a young one about the place, she will be company for me, while you and Fred are busy working."

"Do you think people might gossip, if you make too much fuss of her?"

Young Fred (who actually wasn't that young anymore, having just celebrated his 40th birthday) spoke gently. He knew how sensitive the older man was.

"Perhaps we could compromise. She could have a bedroom downstairs, next to mine and Sybil's, and then spend her days up here with you, like a companion."

It had already been decided (and on this point the old man was adamant) that Daisy would not, under any circumstances, be treated as a servant in his house.

He had smiled at Fred as he said.

"If I had my way neither would you, I think of you as my friends."

Although the remark had been addressed to both of them, Sybil was under no illusions. She knew of the great unspoken (publicly, at least) love between the two men and it warmed her heart to see how happy young Fred was.

That boy had had a very hard passage in life and deserved some joy.

So, Daisy was given a room in the basement and the old man sent her and Sybil, to the shops in the West End, to choose furniture and fabrics.

"The girl needs something pretty. She has suffered more than a child ever should. Take her to the Army and Navy Stores, or Gamages, Harrods, or Swan and Edgar. I have accounts at all of them, so just buy whatever she needs. But no cheap rubbish, you know how fussy I am."

He was very fussy. He had grown up in a stately home in the Cotswolds, a house full of antiques.

His father, Earl Palmer, had been very vocal in his disapproval of his youngest son's sexuality and had threatened to cut him off without a penny "unless you get yourself a wife and father some children, then you can do what you want with your life, society will ignore any indiscretions."

When his father died, it turned out that he had indeed disinherited his son, leaving the estate and all his wealth, to the two elder boys and not even a silver teaspoon to his youngest.

Fortunately, Fredericks mother was independently wealthy and unusually for those days, had managed to retain her personal fortune on marriage.

She came from a family of rich Jewish bankers and lawyers, so they had ensured the money could remain in her direct lineage.

By the time his father died, Frederick was independently wealthy anyway, so the old man's spite did not really matter. It hurt of course, as it had always hurt ,when his father called him a fag, a pansy boy, a sodomite.

He had risen above all this, and the dreadful bullying he had suffered at boarding school, to become a world renowned antiques dealer. Consequently, his home was filled with the most glorious antiques, art, sculpture and furniture from around the globe.

Sybil and Daisy had a wonderful time, shopping for treasures for Daisy's room.

They bought a brass bed, a rosewood dressing table and chest, a cane and wicker chair and a Persian carpet. They ordered yards of exquisite silk fabric to make curtains and bed coverings and a beautiful china jug and bowl set in pink and ivory. They bought clothes galore, bodices and camisoles trimmed with lace, nightdresses of the softest cotton lawn, yards of fabric to be made into dresses, a blue velvet cape with a fur trim, kid gloves, button boots and a pile of lace edged handkerchiefs.

Daisy was completely overcome. She had never set foot in the West End before, her walks with Maisy had always ended before they reached "the posh bit." The huge department stores, with their beautiful shiny wares seemed like heaven to her.

"And the master said I was to make sure you had a few fripperies."

Sybil hadn't been too sure what he meant by that, but was too embarrassed to ask. Fred had explained that it just meant unnecessary, luxury things.

Well, the stores had plenty of those.

"More fripperies than you could wish for if you lived a thousand years." Sybil thought.

In the end, they settled on a hairbrush set made from tortoiseshell, bone and pearl and a Bonbonniere, a small bowl made from fluted glass, with a pretty gilt and enamel lid.

They were both quite exhausted after so much shopping.

And so began the pattern of Daisy's new life. A life of unimaginable luxury for a girl from the slums. But she adapted to it incredibly well.

Frederick Palmer firmly believed that the only reason God had given him such a privileged life, was so that he could share his good fortune with others.

And he tried his very best.

As well as caring for Fred, Daisy, Sybil and all his other servants, he gave generously to many charities and never walked past a beggar on the street without emptying his pockets. He always tipped the carriage drivers and waiters and ensured that

Sybil had enough spare cash in the housekeeping budget, to give the delivery boys a few coins.

Sometimes he bought 4 or 5 newspapers a day, from different ragged urchins selling them on street corners, and the basement kitchen was often filled with waifs and strays he had invited back "for a good hot meal."

Fred often travelled overseas with him, acting as his valet, and he noticed that his master was just as generous when he was abroad.

"He is such a good man" Fred thought "He doesn't just give when people are watching, he doesn't do it for the glory, he does it because he really cares."

So it was a very happy household and Daisy thrived.

Frederick taught her how to play the piano and how to play chess.

He taught her how to dress and behave like a lady.

How to recognise and appreciate art and antiques.

But most of all, she learnt from him how to be kind, to treat others as you would like to be treated.

She was a kind, loving girl anyway, so it wasn't a hard lesson to learn.

The only thing he didn't teach her was how to read and write.

None of them knew that she couldn't.

It took the coalman to work that out.

Sidney John Bacon was the coalman in question.

Otherwise known as Blackie, he had been born into a very poor family.

He had only ever known hardship.

He had only been 13 when his mother died in childbirth, struggling to bring her 14th baby into the world. Both her and the baby had died.

Blackie would never forget the look of utter despair on his father's face, because although their life had been impossibly hard in the slums, it had been a true love match.

"One day I want to love someone like that," he thought.

He was 15 years old when he first started working at the coal yard.

It was hard, back breaking work, shovelling the coal into hundredweight sacks. The weight had to be just right and sometimes, if the coal was too big, he had to use a hammer to break it up. But he worked hard and was ambitious and by the time he was 21 he had been promoted to delivery driver.

He drove his horse and cart, stacked full of bags of coal, all round London. There were six coalmen delivering for the company. They were all older than him, and had been doing it for years, but after a while Blackie was given the Marylebone route, as it seemed that the wealthy customers there appreciated his polite, quiet, and very efficient service. Often their servants invited him into the kitchen for a drink, after he had poured the coal into their cellars, or stacked it neatly in their coal sheds.

The mansion in Montague Street had a coal hole in the pavement outside, with a chute to pour the bags directly into.

This meant he didn't have to disturb anyone, but afterwards, he always knocked on the kitchen door, just to let them know he had been.

"Come on in Blackie. The kettles on and I've just made a fresh batch of cakes, would you like one?"

Sybil was always so kind. He had been delivering coal to the mansion for four years now, and every time, she seemed to have just baked something delicious, almost as if she had been expecting him.

He took off his hat as he walked into the basement kitchen.

It was a bulky thing, as it had a big leather flap, to protect his back and shoulders, as he carried the heavy sacks.

"Thank you. That's so kind of you ma'am"

"Will your horse be alright out there Blackie?"

One of the young kitchen maids blushed as she spoke. She had always been rather taken with the handsome young man.

"Oh, Yes thanks, Mabel. He's used to hanging around waiting for me and anyway I've got a lad with me today, learning the ropes, so he'll keep an eye out."

"Well, when you leave, you must take the lad some cakes too."

They were all chatting away, when Blackie suddenly looked up and saw her.

"The most beautiful thing I have ever seen" he thought.

He stood up, suddenly aware of his filthy clothes and soot stained face and hands. Although he had given them a quick wash before sitting down to eat the cake, he was only too aware that it would take a very long time, standing at the sink tonight, before he would get rid of the smell and grime of the coal.

“Oh hello” the beautiful creature said.

“I just popped down to my room to get a shawl, it’s a bit chilly upstairs.”

“Ok my love, I should use your blue one, the other is prettier, but not so warm.”

With a smile, she was gone. And Blackie felt as though his heart had been pulled from his chest.

“That lass” said Sybil

“I bet she’s been sitting at that piano, with the window open for hours, wonder she doesn’t get a chill.”

If Blackie had realised that Daisy was the family treasure, loved by upstairs and downstairs alike, he would never have had the nerve to pursue her, but as she obviously lived downstairs with the servants, it never occurred to him that she might be out of his reach.

Although Daisy had seemed unaware of his presence, she had actually noticed the tall, handsome young coalman. Having casually asked Fred how often their coal was delivered, she took to appearing in the kitchen every Tuesday and Friday at 2 o’clock.

“Here, do you think our Daisy likes him?” Mabel enquired of Sybil.

“What on earth are you talking about, girl?”

“Do you think our Daisy likes the coalman?”

Sybil was horrified and spoke to Fred.

“But, Fred, we must protect her. She’s only 17 and knows nothing of the world. And anyway, what would the master say?”

That evening, the two men were in the library as usual, lounging and drinking whisky, wearing their matching smoking jackets. The older man had bought them as a surprise gift at Christmas. They were splendid things, made of brown velvet, lined with Scotch Paisley and with a quilted collar and cuffs of brown satin. Young Fred had been quite overcome.

"My dear boy, you know how much you mean to me and at least when we wear these, on our evenings together here, it feels like we belong to each other."

"Fred?"

The younger man spoke hesitantly, unsure where to begin.

"Yes my dear?"

"It seems as if our Daisy has developed an affection for a young man."

"Oh my God, who?"

"His name is Sidney, but they call him Blackie."

"And who is he? What does he do? Is he good enough for our girl? "

"Don't you think she is a bit young to be thinking of anything like that?"

Fred agreed wholeheartedly. If he had his way, Daisy would never be allowed to leave the house alone, and certainly never with a man!

And so the following week, the older man also happened to be in the kitchen on Tuesday afternoon, just as they heard the coal being poured into the chute outside.

He stood up as Blackie entered the kitchen and went over and shook his hand.

"Good day young man, please forgive me for never greeting you until today."

"I understand from Fred, that you have been doing a splendid job, delivering our coal for the last 4 years."

Blackie stood there, wringing his hat in his sooty hands, looking quite uncomfortable.

"Thank you sir."

None of them failed to notice the way he kept glancing across to where Daisy sat. Or the way she smiled shyly back at him.

They were married the following summer.

Daisy was just 18 and Blackie was 25.

He had received a lot of advice from both the Freds, and Sybil, on how he should conduct himself as her husband. He was also under threat of death, from all of them, should he treat her badly.

They were married in church, with everyone they loved watching. It was an exceptionally happy occasion.

At the wedding breakfast afterwards, back at the house, Blackie proudly showed off their marriage certificate. He still couldn't believe that this beautiful girl was really his wife.

The bride and groom had retired for the night, to their new home next door. Frederick had given them the Mews Cottage as a wedding present.

That way Daisy would still be close by, so they could all check on her regularly.

"What a wonderful day."

He had invited Sybil to join him and Fred in the library.

She had worked so hard for the last week, preparing a delicious feast to celebrate the wedding, but he knew that she would be feeling sad, now that their girl had left the house for ever.

"Yes, it certainly was, but something is troubling me"

"Did either of you look closely at the marriage certificate?"

"Did you notice that Daisy just made her mark, didn't sign her name?"

The next day, when Daisy and Blackie called round for lunch, he asked them upstairs.

"You come too, Fred and Sybil."

No one had realised that Daisy couldn't read or write.

She had been such a bright, sunny little girl, who had just wanted to please, and so none of them had noticed that she never actually read or wrote anything. She had learnt to play the piano by ear and just pretended to read the books in the library.

Her mother, Polly, had been fiercely ambitious for her daughter.

Having grown up in the Workhouse herself, she had been determined that her little girl would have a better life. But she had died before Daisy was three years old, before she had the opportunity to teach her anything.

And then Daisy lived in the slums until she was 13, and although Maisy and John were kind and loving, they were not academic.

There had been no books in the house and certainly no money to buy any. And of course, she had never been sent to school.

"You have lived in my home for 5 years and I didn't notice."

"I am so ashamed of myself."

"Please forgive me Daisy."

"We've known you all your life, and we didn't notice either love."

Sybil and Fred were both choked up.

She ran across the room and flung her arms around the three of them in turn.

"You have absolutely nothing to apologise for. You have all given me the most wonderful life. Without all of you, I would be nothing."

"Dead in a ditch somewhere probably."

And then she burst into tears.

Blackie, who was looking very smart, in a crisp, white shirt and dark suit, rushed over to his bride and held her tightly, while she sobbed.

After a while, everyone calmed down, thanks in part to a nip of brandy, which Frederick explained was strictly for medicinal purposes.

Blackie spoke softly, while stroking Daisy's hair to calm her.

"I didn't mean for anyone to get upset. I just thought you all knew."

"But how did you find out?"

"Did she tell you herself?"

"Not exactly."

"We were in the park one day and she asked me to pick her some flowers."

"I teased her and said I would, if she spelt out the names of the flowers she wanted."

"She burst into tears and told me she couldn't."

"Because she couldn't read. Or write."

There was a stunned silence in the room.

"But don't worry, because I am going to make sure all my babies can read and write, as soon as they are big enough."

Their first born daughter, Florence, arrived the following year.

She was born in the Mews Cottage, in a flurry of excitement, quite different to her mother Daisy's arrival in the slums, just 19 years previously.

And by the time Florence was four years old, Blackie had taught both his wife and his daughter, to read and write.

ALABAMA
1919

Theo and Melissa had been married in the Spring of 1919.

There had seemed little point in having a long engagement.

Both sets of parents were delighted to be getting their troublesome offspring off their hands at last and they were both very sure of their feelings, so why wait?

Of course they had had to endure a grand society wedding, which they both hated.

Held in the manicured grounds of Melissa's family home, it had been a magnificent occasion, with huge elaborate floral arrangements everywhere and lots of small excited children, running around the lawns eating wedding cake.

Theo was quiet all day. He just wanted to get away from it all and be alone with his new wife. But mostly he was angry that Matty wasn't there.

Matty was his best friend and he had wanted him to be his best man.

"For God's sake boy. Do you want us to be the laughing stock of the county?"

"One of your brothers will do the job. Be much more suitable."

He had argued with his father. So loudly that they heard him in the old slave quarters.

"At least you know he tried, my boy." Old Freddie spoke kindly.

He could see how heartbroken his grandson was, at being excluded from his friend's special day.

Just because he was black.

"Nothing has really changed, even though we ain't slaves no more" he thought sadly to himself.

"At least you're gonna go with Master Theo to his new home, they'll be happier times there, I'm sure."

He had met Melissa on several occasions since the engagement and thought she was perfect for the young master. He had always worried about the boy. Since he was quite small, he had chosen to spend most of his free time in Old Freddie's cabin in the old slave quarters and had often said that he wished he could live there, with them, all the time.

Theo's belief that everyone should be equal, whether they were Black or White, or rich or poor, and his refusal to see women and servants as mere chattels, was very badly received in the big house, but much appreciated by his friends in the old slave quarters.

And it seemed that his bride shared exactly the same views.

"Their world is so small, they don't care what happens outside their little bubble here in Alabama."

"Well of course, my sisters are interested in the latest Paris and London fashions and need to know what the best dressed ladies in New York are wearing. But apart from that they don't give a fig about what's going on in the world. It will be such a relief to get away from them all and have some decent conversation."

"For such a small, pretty person, she sure does have a lot to say" thought the old man.

But he was delighted that the boy had found such a fine wife and he knew that Matty thought the same. He was going to miss them all, but they had promised to come back every week to visit him.

Melissa' father had wanted them to live in the big family house in Tuskegee, but she had refused.

"Oh Daddy, you know I love you and I will always be your little girl, but Theo and I want our own place."

As they had both grown up protected by their families fortunes and had never had to work, they were now in the uncomfortable position of being reliant on their parents for a future home.

"His Daddy has offered us a small guest house on their plantation, but you know I really want to stay here, close by. I would be so lonesome without you all."

She knew exactly how to wind her father around her little finger and was sure that by telling him about her future father in laws offer, she would get what she wanted.

What she and Theo wanted, was the little house right on the edge of her father's plantation. Far enough away from the family, so that they could live their own life. It was a lovely little house in the Steamboat Gothic style, with wide porches on every side. Not as grand as her sisters' houses on the estate, but certainly big enough for her and Theo, and their babies when they came. She wanted at least six.

Matty was moving in with them of course and so was Ruth, Melissa's maid, who had looked after her since she was a baby. The others, like the gardeners and the house-maids, would not live in, but would walk across the fields every day to help them. They planned to do all their own cooking.

On the day of the wedding, her father handed Theo the deeds to the little house.

"I hope you understand, son, why I have put it in just my girl's name. In case anything happened to me. I don't want her having to fight her sisters just to keep her home."

Of course Theo understood. And he was delighted that his new father in law was treating Melissa as an equal, a person in her own right, not just an appendage to her new husband.

So it all started very well.

While they were on their honeymoon in Huntsville, Matty and Ruth moved in and prepared the new house for their return.

In Huntsville, they revelled in their new found freedom,

They spent hours, just exploring and enjoying each other, in their suite at the Huntsville Inn, on the Main Square. They took a carriage ride around the town and marvelled at all the beautiful old homes, mostly large white Antebellum-style houses. They were certainly splendid, gracious old mansions, but they were horrified to see all the old slave quarters, still there in the gardens. They were mostly freshly painted, to match the grand houses and probably used as storerooms or sheds. It broke both their hearts to think of all the misery those little shacks had witnessed.

When they finally got back to their new home in Tuskegee, they were upset to see that Matty and Ruth had moved into two of the old slave cabins on the property.

"But we want you to live in the house with us, like family" Melissa sounded tearful.

"Yes, absolutely, let's start this new life off how we mean to continue"

Theo was emotional.

"You two are our family now."

And so the very next morning, Theo, Matty and the two gardeners, pulled down the old shacks and Matty and Ruth moved into their own rooms in the main house. Neither of them had ever known such luxury before.

Mellisa's and Theo's families were horrified of course.

"Such useful little buildings, where on earth will your servants sleep now?"

It became such a happy home. They didn't get many visitors (which actually suited them very well) because people were so scandalised by their living arrangements.

"Can you believe they let their servants live in the main house with them?" "And I understand they even eat all their meals together, at the same table."

And that is exactly what they did.

Ruth taught Melissa how to cook and she became surprisingly good at it. Occasionally she would let Theo help, but the kitchen very quickly became her domain.

"Darling Theo, I am 19 years old and this is the first time I have ever been allowed to do my own cooking. If you had ever really wanted to, I'm quite sure you could have managed to cook, sometime in the 32 years you've been alive."

Theo burst out laughing.

"How did I ever manage to find someone like you?"

"You are the loveliest, most intelligent and interesting woman I have ever met. And the most beautiful, kind and passionate one too!"

Melissa blushed.

Despite their age difference and her complete lack of experience, she had indeed proved to be passionate. And she adored everything about him.

Their evenings were very jolly. Once they had eaten dinner, the four of them would sit on the front porch and watch the sun going down.

Sometimes they just chatted and Theo and Matty would recount all their adventures to the girls. They talked about the places they had been, the fine cities, the architecture they had marvelled at, the different food they had eaten. But most of all they talked about the people they had met.

They didn't talk about all the women of course.

"When we were in London, we heard the tale of an escaped slave called Jacob Cummings. My ears pricked up, because he had the same name as me.

Of course slaves used to have to carry their master's name. I don't know if he had once been on our plantation, but his account of how he escaped to freedom moved me mightily."

"And Matty and I were horrified when we visited the Cotton Mills in England."

"Weren't we Matty?"

"Those poor people work in hell holes, dirty dangerous work and are very poorly paid. And even small children have to work in those awful conditions, it is so wrong."

Ruth looked across at Matty and smiled. She knew that he was thinking the exact same thing as her. How lucky they both were to be here, in this place, with these two, wonderful, caring people.

She had always known how Melissa felt about equality. She had taken care of her all her life, in fact sometimes she felt as though the girl was her own, the child she had never had. She was 30 years old now and had been with Melissa since she was just 11, a child herself. Never in her wildest dreams had she ever imagined that one day she would live in the same house, as her equal.

"Why do they choose not to see that we are all the same. The colour of our skin, or whether we were born rich or poor, should not make any difference to how we are treated in this life."

Melissa spoke with such passion, that the other three smiled.

They had heard her say this so many times.

As if they, of all people, needed convincing.

"Well, that more or less is what Harriet said."

Harriet Tubman, the famous anti — slavery abolitionist, was Melissa's hero.

She often quoted her.

Theo had given Melissa a beautiful leather bound copy of "Uncle Tom's Cabin" written by Harriet Beacher — Stowe, as a wedding present.

She had always loved the book, but had hesitated to tell him what her heroine, the other Harriet, had said about it:

"I've heard Uncle Tom's Cabin read, and I tell you Mrs Stowe's pen hasn' begun to paint what slavery is as I have seen it at the far South. I've seen de real thing, and I don't want to see it on no stage or in no theater."

Some evenings, they got out the Isle of Lewis chess set that Theo had bought in London. Mostly he and Matty played, while the girls sat and talked, but occasionally they tried to teach them.

Ruth was very smart and quickly understood all the different moves, but Melissa was too impatient to concentrate properly.

"Oh these damn bishops and pawns, they may look lovely, but it is impossible to remember what to do with them."

And then, one bright and sunny day, when the fields were white with cotton waiting to be picked, when they had been married for only one year, Theo suddenly died.

His heart just gave out.

And Melissa's heart was broken into a thousand pieces.

They had had so many plans, so many dreams, and now he was gone.

Before they had achieved all they wanted to do.

Before they had even managed to make a baby.

After Theo died, Melissa wept for months.

She dragged herself around, couldn't eat or sleep, and every time someone mentioned his name, she went pale and left the room.

Matty and Ruth were at their wits end. They too had loved him passionately and were devastated by his loss. He had been a very fine man, who treated them with love and respect and they missed him dreadfully.

Melissa's parents had begged her to go home, back to the big house.

"Absolutely not", she told them, with tears pouring down her pretty face.

"This is my home now, even with my darling gone. I can't just go back to my old life now and anyway Matty and Ruth are here to look after me."

For a whole year after Theo died, they barely left the house.

Melissa would often sit on the porch, staring into space for hours on end. Hoping that if she concentrated hard enough, her beloved husband would come marching across the fields.

Heartbroken as she was, she was determined not to give up and go back to her parents house. She would be stifled there, living her old life. Living a lie.

So they stayed in the little house and gradually their grief lessened.

They found comfort in his books and read and reread his journals, almost as if by reliving his life, they could bring him back to them.

Matty told the girls stories of their travels, of all the adventures he and Theo had had during their 5 years away. He was a fine story teller and they imagined themselves in Paris, Rome, Venice or London.

"Please tell us again about Hannibal and the elephants. Did you ride them?"

Matty laughed, the first time he had laughed properly since his friend died.

"Oh Ruth, that happened years ago, hundreds and hundreds of years ago." "Theo and I just crossed the Alps using the same route as Hannibal did."

After a year of public mourning, Melissa stopped wearing black.

But she didn't stop grieving.

She had sent Matty to the jeweller in Montgomery to have a mourning ring made. It was a beautiful thing, made of gold and jet and it contained a lock of Theo's hair. His name and the date of his death were inscribed on the inside.

"I shall wear this every day, until the day I die. It is all I have left of my darling."

Once the period of official mourning was over, they began to get more visitors.

She was a pretty and rich young widow, so of course suitors came running.

"Like rats out of a burning barn," she thought.

"Not willing to stick around unless I jump into their arms instantly, just here for the spoils."

And worse, some of them were really rude and disrespectful to Matty and Ruth, treating them like slaves.

"Even if I wanted another husband, I would never give those dreadful men even my hand to kiss."

She also had a couple of visits from an old friend of her fathers, a man she had never liked much, who she knew was a leading member of the local branch of the Ku Klux Klan.

"My dear child. My wife and I would like you to come and stay with us for a while. Just until you feel yourself again and find a good man to look after you. We can't have you staying here, with such unsuitable living arrangements."

Melissa was furious, but she didn't argue. There was no point and anyway, she had been brought up to respect her elders, however rude and bigoted they may be.

But how dare he be so disrespectful to her Ruth and Matty.

They were worth 100 times more than he would ever be.

That evening, after dinner, when the three of them were sitting on the porch and Matty was reading to them from Theo's journal, she had an inspiration.

"Why don't we take a trip? Go on a little adventure. Retrace your footsteps."

It was the first time since Theo had died that she had felt any real emotion, other than raw grief and anger.

LONDON
1921

While Melissa was in Alabama, planning her big adventure, life continued much the same in Montague Place.

Everyone was well and content.

Daisy and Blackie were still very happy together and life in the little Mews Cottage was full of joy and laughter.

They had both been hoping for a big family, but sadly two of their babies (both boys) were stillborn. Not even Frederick's expensive doctors could save them. They were all heartbroken, but at least they still had their lovely Florence.

She was now 15 years old and the light of all of their lives.

Instead of her mother and grandmother's beautiful blonde curls, she had inherited Blackie's thick, almost jet black, hair.

She was not exactly pretty, her features were not classically beautiful like Daisy's, but she was stunning.

With her green eyes and winning smile, she was incredibly attractive.

And she was tall, so tall.

No-one knew where her height had come from, she was almost six feet tall and towered over them all.

"Perhaps her great-grandmother was tall?"

No-one would ever know for sure, as her great-grandmother had died giving birth to her daughter Polly (Daisy's mum) in the Workhouse. And Polly had died when Daisy was tiny. They had never been able to trace any other family. Frederick had tried to find out, but the Workhouse records had been destroyed.

Such a lot had happened in the last few years.

Not to them, but to the world in general.

Old Queen Victoria had died of course and for a while it seemed like the country would never get over losing the old girl.

Her eldest son, Edward V11, known as Bertie, reigned for the next 9 years, living extravagantly. He was rather too fond of the ladies, leading his wife, the lovely Queen Alexandra, a merry dance.

When he died in 1910, he had been replaced by his brother George V, a quite different character, who with his wife Queen Mary, were ruling the country in a much more Victorian manner.

There there had been all the troubles in Russia, and the dreadful 1906 San Francisco earthquake with so many lives lost. Then in 1912 the Titanic sank on its maiden voyage.

And from 1914 to 1918, so many brave men and women had perished in the Great War, the war to end all wars. That was followed by the Spanish Flu pandemic, where more than 20 million people died.

And then the last Emperor of Russia, Tsar Nicholas, and his entire family, were assassinated.

The first part of the new century had not been an easy one.

But now they were in a new decade, the 1920s, and hopefully it would be better for everyone.

Frederick Palmer was now well into his seventies, but still fit and strong. It helped of course that he could afford to consult the best doctors and had never had any money worries. In fact he often thought he had led a very charmed existence, especially since young Fred had become part of his life.

Young Fred was now middle aged, but the two men were as close as ever.

They had always been very discreet about their friendship, so although there were odd whisperings, only Sybil knew the truth.

She was not so young now either, but still ran the kitchen, even though she let the younger maids do a lot of the cooking nowadays.

All three of them spent a lot of time visiting the Mews House.

When Daisy and Blackie were first married, they didn't visit without an invitation, but once Florence arrived they couldn't keep away.

Daisy was always pleased to see them, to help with the little one and to keep her company.

Blackie worked very long hours, especially since Frederick had given him the money to buy his own horse and cart. He left before six every morning to go to the coal yard to load up, and didn't return home till it was dark.

Daisy always had the tin bath ready for him, but by the time he had managed to remove all the soot grime from his face and hands and eat his dinner, he was exhausted and ready for bed. His round now extended from Marylebone right across town to Bloomsbury.

But both he and Daisy were content.

They knew that the only reason he worked so hard, was to ensure his wife and daughter wanted for nothing. They knew how lucky they were not to have to pay rent, Frederick had been so generous, insisting on giving them the Mews Cottage as a wedding present.

Florence, affectionately known by them all as Flo, adored her father, Blackie.

It made Daisy so happy to watch them together. She had never known the joy of having a father, although she always felt that Fred, Frederick and even old John (Maisy's husband from Stepney) had filled that gap in her life.

Flo was a very bright little girl with a sunny nature like her mother.

Frederick had insisted on sending her to a good school and although she had enjoyed the social aspect of it and made some good friends, she was not particularly academic.

"But why do I have to keep reading and writing every day?"

"Dad taught me to read when I was little and I don't need to write letters, so maybe I could just leave school now."

She had been just ten years old when she said this.

And then she discovered her passion. She had been making cakes with Sybil in the kitchen one day.

"Sybil, is it true that my mum used to live here, in that little room next door?"

"Oh love, you know she did, How many times have you asked me that?"

"That was her room from the time she came here, when she was 13, until she married your Dad and moved to the Mews."

"Can I go and have a look?"

Before Sybil had time to answer, Flo had opened the door to Daisy's old room and was sitting on the bed.

"Why do you keep it like this?"

The room was exactly as Daisy had left it on the day she married Blackie and moved next door. She had just taken her clothes, the china jug and bowl and her hairbrush set, to her new home.

But this still felt like her room and she used to pop over and sit in it sometimes. Usually times when she was feeling a bit sad.

Like when her babies had died.

So they had changed nothing in the room, just left it all there for her.

"Can I come and stay here when I'm bigger and I leave home?"

Sybil burst out laughing.

"Don't let your Mum and Dad hear you talking about leaving home. It'll break their hearts."

But Flo wasn't listening.

"What's in this big chest? Can I open it and see?"

She lifted the lid and gasped. It was stuffed, full to the brim, with the most beautiful fabrics. Leftover pieces from the curtains and bedcover and all the dresses they had made for Daisy.

"Oh Sybil, do you think I could make something with all this?"

The older woman stifled a chuckle. The girl had never shown the slightest interest in sewing before. She didn't like the discipline of school much, so was very unlikely to have the patience for needlework.

"Well I guess you could ask your Mum if it's alright."

"Hello my darling girl, what are you doing in here?"

Flo leapt off the bed and rushed into his arms.

"Oh Mr. Palmer. I've just discovered all this beautiful treasure and I want to use it , but Sybil says I have to ask Mum first."

"Well, if Sybil says so, then I think you must."

"But it's your house, you could give me permission."

As she said this, she looked up at him and smiled. Her best, most persuasive smile. And he was lost.

He had loved this child from the first moment he saw her. He had loved her mother Daisy too, from the minute she had set foot in his house when she was just 13 and now he loved her daughter passionately too. As passionately as though she was his own. The child that he and Fred would never have.

"Oh Flo" he said with great affection.

"Why on earth do you want all this old material? I can buy you some new stuff if you like and we can ask the dressmaker to run you up something nice."

She released herself from his embrace and stood upright. She was much taller than him, even though she was only 15.

"Please, I promise I won't waste it. I have big plans."

Obviously he relented and was then persuaded to walk with her, to the Haberdashers, in the High Street, to buy some thread and needles.

They had a wonderful time. There was nothing he wouldn't do for her, so they bought ribbons, lace, pins, needles, a measuring tape and a dear little wicker basket to store them all in.

The very next day she got started. She sat in Daisy's old bedroom for hours. And the next day she came back. And the day after that.

She wouldn't let any of them see what she was doing.

"Oh Mum, I just want it to be a surprise."

After a week had passed she asked them all to come to the kitchen.

She had intended to use the library, but that would have meant showing Mr. Palmer before the others, and that wouldn't have been fair.

It was a Sunday morning.

Blackie's only day off.

The women had been to church, but the two Freds and Blackie had stayed at home. They had been asked to assemble at 12.30. On the dot.

Flo looked around the room. All the people she loved most in the world were there, waiting patiently for her to show them her creation.

She coughed rather theatrically.

"I am delighted you could all come today, to attend my show."

"If you would all care to close your eyes for a minute."

They heard the bedroom door close and then a few minutes later open again.

They gasped in unison.

Their little girl was stunning.

Wearing the most beautiful gown, made of scraps of satin, a muddle of colours, stitched lengthwise so the pieces of fabric hung like petals.

Frederick was the first to recover his senses.

"My darling, darling girl. You look wonderful. Surely you didn't make that exquisite gown yourself?"

Flo coloured. She was thrilled that they liked it.

"Yes, yes I did. And I have so loved doing it. See how good my sewing is."

The dress was long, almost to her calf, so she lifted the hem to show them. Holding it up to each of them in turn.

And they were amazed. It was not just a wonderful, clever design, but the sewing was beautiful. Tiny even stitches, almost invisible to the naked eye.

Flo suddenly realised her Mum was crying.

"Oh Mum, please forgive me, I didn't mean to upset you. I know the material was yours and I didn't ask you. But I did ask Mr. Palmer and he said it would be ok. In fact he even came to the shop and helped me choose all the ribbons and sewing thread and everything."

Her voice trailed off, she had been so excited and now it was all spoilt.

Her Mum was cross with her and probably her Dad was too.

She saw Blackie cross the room and put his arms round her Mum.

"Oh my love, whatever's wrong?"

He knew it wasn't because their girl had used the fabric without her permission. They would both have given their precious daughter the moon if she asked for it.

"It just reminded me of my Mum."

Sybil and Fred both rushed over and Blackie stood aside, so they could hug her. Of course they had both known and loved her mum Polly too. In fact Sybil had been there when she gave birth to Daisy.

"Oh love."

"I know I was only small when she died, but seeing my Flo in that dress just reminded me of her."

"Your mum was the most wonderful seamstress Daisy and I think your Grandmother was too. Apparently she was well known in the workhouse for her beautiful work, that's why she was sent to the Fox-Leightons, to make dresses for the mistress."

No-one had ever told Flo much about her grandmother Polly, or who her Mum's father was. She had asked of course, as children always do, but none of them really wanted to burden her with the truth.

"You must have inherited their talent."

Flo was thrilled. At last she had found something that she was good at and really enjoyed.

Now she could start planning her life.

BEDFORD COURT MANSIONS
BLOOMSBURY
1922

Melissa loved the imposing mansion block where they had chosen to make their new home in London.

Bedford Court Mansions was a fine red brick building, dating back to the 1890's. It was set on Bedford Avenue, a wide, tree lined road.

They had chosen a large mansion flat, set over two floors, the ground floor and the basement, which meant they also had a small paved garden to sit and watch the world pass by. Their apartment was on the corner, and had huge bay windows which flooded the rooms with light. It was the perfect place. Grand, but not too grand, and no maintenance to worry about. There were even porters to help with anything you might need.

She had persuaded her father to pay the rent in advance for a 5 year lease.

"Please Daddy. I am still only 22 and five years is not long. If I haven't found a rich husband after that, I can always come home."

Of course she had absolutely no intention of ever going back to Alabama and definitely never planned to marry again, but she did need his financial support.

It had started off as just an idea, a little adventure to cheer them all up after Theo's premature death.

Her family were totally against it of course, the thought of her gallivanting around Europe with just Matty and Ruth, was too much for them to bear.

But she was adamant.

"If you insist, I will just stay here and rot. I will never, ever, remarry and I will just become a miserable old lady."

Her parents loved her dearly and so they eventually and very reluctantly agreed.

"How I wish I could be my own woman Matty and not have to rely on my father for every penny. Then I could just go whenever I felt like it."

Her father had insisted that they travel to England on one of the Cunard liners "The Berengaria".

"It is a fine ship my dear. Was built in Germany in 1912 and seized by the Allies after the war and turned into a luxury transatlantic vessel. They built it with a second skin around the hull, so it wouldn't sink like the Titanic."

So, on a fine spring day in 1922 they had sailed from New York, bound for Southampton, England.

Melissa had been beside herself with excitement.

Her father had booked them a stateroom on the First Class deck.

Initially, he had wanted Matty and Ruth to travel on one of the lower decks, but she was adamant they must be with her.

"Daddy, I will feel so much safer on that big ship, if they have rooms right next to mine."

Of course she wasn't frightened at all, just furious that her father still tried to treat them as second class citizens. But she had learnt over the years that the best way to get what she wanted from him was to act like a sweet little girl.

The ship was indeed magnificent, well the First Class deck was, at least.

Their stateroom was huge, with a bedroom for each of them. No expense had been spared in the public rooms either, with beautiful dining rooms, the Palm Court and even an "English Tudor style Smoking Room" for the gentlemen passengers. They enjoyed bracing strolls around the windy decks and marvelled at the special launching system for the lifeboats. One of the ships officers explained that it had an independent lighting system, that wasn't reliant on the engine room in case of emergencies. And apparently there were sufficient lifeboats on every deck. Unlike on the fated Titanic.

The trip only took 5 days, which amazed her. She had read stories where just 100 years ago, the same journey had taken 15 long days.

The only thing which spoilt the experience for her, was the attitude of some of their fellow passengers.

The first evening they were at sea, there was a Captain's Welcome Cocktail Party.

They made a splendid entrance.

The beautiful young widow, in a plum coloured silk gown, that accentuated her slim figure, together with her two friends.

Matty looked incredibly handsome in his black dinner suit and white shirt, while Ruth was wearing a long dress of pale yellow satin, which seemed to ripple as she walked.

You could almost hear the gasps as they took their allocated seats at the Captains table.

None of them could fail to notice the disapproving stares.

At the end of the evening, as they got up to leave, one of the passengers at the next table came over.

"My dear Mrs Cummings, may I have a private word with you?"

Matty and Ruth began to walk to the door.

"My dear, I know this is your first time on such a splendid liner and you probably are not yet quite familiar with everything, but I do feel that perhaps you should insist that your staff stay in their cabins at mealtimes. Their presence in the dining room has been causing some distress amongst the other passengers."

Melissa was speechless. She had not realised that racial prejudice was still as rife amongst the English aristocracy, as it had been in her native Alabama.

She could see that Matty and Ruth were looking uncomfortable. In fact Ruth looked very close to tears.

"I regret sir, that some of our fellow passengers find our company intolerable."

"Please assure them that my friends and I, find their behaviour and attitude to be absolutely despicable. I have no servants, these are my friends and I would have expected an English gentleman to have treated them with more respect."

With that she sailed past him and the three of them returned to their stateroom.

And every evening, for the remainder of the voyage, she insisted that they went back into the magnificent dining room for dinner.

Matty was used to such treatment, he had suffered from it when he and Theo were travelling, but Ruth had never left the plantation before.

"Whatever I do, however fine I dress, it's always gonna be the same."

"Just because my face is black, they are always gonna treat me like a slave."

"Well that may be so Ruth, but I am damned if I am going to let them get away with it. We are not going to just hide away in our cabins. My Daddy paid a lot of money for our passages and that makes us their equals."

Matty smiled. Sometimes she sounded just like Theo.

How he missed his friend. If only he had been with them on this trip, no-one would have dared talk to them like that.

They all enjoyed the Transatlantic crossing, but the shine had rather gone from it, due to such open hostility, so none of them were too sad to disembark in Southampton.

The next day they caught the train to London and the girls marvelled as the green countryside flashed by. The pretty little villages with their thatched cottages, the rows of red brick houses, their yards almost touching the train tracks. And then they reached London, a vast metropolis of solid, splendid buildings, wide tree lined streets, fine shops and beautifully dressed people.

Her father had booked them into a hotel in Mayfair, the same one he always used when he travelled to England to visit the cotton mills.

It was a very fine establishment, perfectly situated for exploring the city.

After just 2 weeks, she had decided that London should be their new home.

"I think we should try Bloomsbury. They say it is much more modern and bohemian and property is cheaper there."

They had met some very interesting people during their stay at the hotel.

Some of the more enlightened ones had realised that they would find it easier to blend into London society, somewhere slightly less formal than Mayfair. They understood only too well, that if Melissa had been a rich young widow living alone, she would have been more socially acceptable.

The three of them had settled very well into their new home. They loved its proximity to all that the city had to offer. They could walk to the shops in the West End, to the theatres, the Royal Opera House in Covent Garden, the parks. They wandered for hours round the streets, just admiring the architecture.

"Oh I do wish Theo was here with us, that would make it just perfect."

They often went to the British Museum, just around the corner in Great Russell Street, or the Victoria and Albert Museum and the Science Museum in Kensington.

They made new friends. People who accepted them for who they were, who enjoyed hearing about their old lives in Alabama and admired them for being brave enough to change things.

It was the Roaring Twenties, a time of great change, both here and in America.

There was more economic stability in both countries, after the upheaval of the Great War, although Prohibition had been introduced in America, which meant it was now illegal to sell or consume alcohol there.

"Thank goodness we don't have to go to a speakeasy to have a "Bees Knees".

This was their favourite cocktail of the moment. A mixture of gin, honey and lemon juice.

Last week it had been a "Highball."

They were entertaining a few friends, before going to a nightclub to listen to the latest jazz band. Apart from cocktails, the conversation shifted from poetry, to art, to politics and back to jazz, depending on the speaker.

Their new friends were a very eclectic and exotic bunch.

Most of the women had their hair bobbed in the latest style, but because Melissa and Ruth both had curly hair, they had opted for a Marcel Wave. Cut short, into the nape of their neck, this accentuated their beautiful features.

They were both wearing the latest "Flapper Girl" dresses, Melissa's was a stunning navy blue silk with a fringed bottom and rhinestones around the neckline.

Ruth looked simply stunning in a fuschia pink one, with black fringes and beading. The men could barely take their eyes off either of them.

Matty was so proud of them both.

But he felt something else too. It was almost as if he was seeing Ruth properly, for the first time.

He watched her all evening.

When she danced with the other men in their group, swaying her hips in time to the music, he wanted to run over and grab her out of their arms.

He suddenly realised that the deep feelings he had for her and had had,ever since they left Alabama, were much more than friendship. Maybe it was just the music, the jazz with its deep African roots, affecting him?

"Melissa, what would you think, if I told you I thought I was in love with Ruth?"

He and Melissa were alone the next day, in the basement kitchen.

Ruth had gone to town to collect some fabric to make them new dresses.

"Oh Matty, I am thrilled."

"I had always hoped that you two would get together, you are just perfect for each other."

"But do you think she likes me?"

She looked at him and smiled.

"Matty, any woman in the world would be lucky to have you. If I was ever going to get married again, it would certainly have been to you."

They were still laughing, when Ruth came back and she eyed them both suspiciously.

"What in the lord's name are you two up to now?"

Matty and Ruth were married just a few weeks later.

Melissa insisted on sending them on honeymoon, a little trip to the seaside at Brighton. They came back looking as happy and content as any newly-wed couple would, and for a few minutes she couldn't stop her tears.

"How I miss my Theo." she thought sadly.

Life settled back into its comfortable pattern. As well as the letter of credit her father had given her when she left home, he also paid the rent on their apartment and gave her a monthly allowance, which was more than enough to provide them with a comfortable lifestyle.

"Now I have a wife, I would like to contribute to the bills."

"The club has offered me a job playing with the band, just a couple of nights a week, but good money."

One of their friends had lent him a saxophone and they were all amazed how quickly and easily he had learnt to play it. And he played it very well.

"I know they only want me because I'm Black and incredibly handsome."

His wife poked him affectionately and Melissa laughed.

"I think that's wonderful Matty and at least you know we will always be in the audience cheering you on. Just think how many new dresses we'll need if we are going out every night."

Ruth had been making all their dresses. This was her way of contributing and Melissa knew it was important to both of them, to feel they weren't just living off her Daddy's money.

They had soon realised that all the beautiful clothes they had brought with them from America, were not really suitable for their new life. They were far too fussy and structured.

No-one in London wore corsets anymore, those horrible constricting undergarments that you had to be laced into and then could barely breathe.

Instead, they wore shorter and lighter clothing, dresses with drop waists, made of silk, satin, cotton or velvet. And matching Cloche hats.

With long pearl necklaces and sharp geometric patterned or sparkly diamond or paste jewellery.

They went to all the Mannequin Shows held at the big West End department stores to get their ideas and then bought yards and yards of fabric, to make their own clothes.

Ruth was an excellent dressmaker, but Melissa was too impatient to sit sewing for hours and soon got bored.

"Oh Ruth, I do feel bad that you end up doing all the work and I just get to enjoy them." "Perhaps we should find another dressmaker to help you?"

LONDON
1922

Since Florence had discovered she could sew, she had spent almost every waking hour doing so.

Sybil and Daisy both had three new dresses each.

The two Freds had beautiful new waistcoats, made of navy blue wool, with red paisley linings.

For her father, Blackie, she had made a smoking jacket of the softest black velvet, with dark green silk quilted collar and cuffs.

"It will be lovely and cosy after your bath Dad, when you come in from work all worn out and tired."

She loved her father passionately and hated it that he worked so hard, coming home every evening exhausted, from lugging heavy sacks of coal around all day. He had a boy to help him now, but his round had grown bigger. The rich folk in the big houses of Marylebone and Bloomsbury appreciated his quiet, honest efficiency.

He could have given it up, old Frederick had often suggested he become his chauffeur instead, but Blackie had politely refused the offer.

"My darling girl"

Even after all these years, he still adored Daisy, his wife, with a passion.

"The old man has been so good to us, but enough is enough."

"He gave us this house and has been so good to our girl."

"Look how he indulges this sewing craze of hers, they seem to be up West every other day, buying rolls of fabric."

It was true.

Old Frederick indulged Florence, in exactly the same way he had always indulged Daisy. Nothing was too much trouble for his girls.

A lesser man than Blackie might have resented it, another man being able to give his family more than he could. But Blackie understood. He understood that Daisy and Flo, Sybil and young Fred, even himself, were the family the old man had never been able to have.

His sexual preferences meant that he would never know the joys of fatherhood.

So Blackie was more than happy to share his girls.

His refusal of the chauffeurs job, meant that the old man had offered it to young Fred instead. They appointed a new butler and now the two men could spend much more time together, driving around London and taking little jaunts into the countryside.

Frederick bought a Rolls Royce Silver Ghost automobile, one of the finest cars available.

The bodywork was light grey and the upholstery was black leather. It was a splendid car, an open tourer and admired by all who saw it.

He refused to let Fred wear a uniform.

"You are my friend, not my servant, and people will just have to get used to it."

Blackie delivered coal to the Bedford Court Mansions every Tuesday afternoon.

Usually he just poured the coal into the chute, in the pavement outside, and then knocked on the basement kitchen door, to let them know he had been.

This particular Tuesday was a warm and sunny Spring day and he could hear voices in the basement garden.

"Oh Blackie, is that you?"

Matty liked the coalman.

He was always polite and respectful and never left any coal dust on the pavement.

"Do come down and have a cold drink with us, you must be parched."

A woman's voice spoke, not one he recognised.

He rubbed his grubby hand across his face. Black soot was etched into the deep creases.

Leaving the boy with the cart, reminding him to hold tight to the horse's reins, he descended the stone steps.

A very pretty young woman stood up to greet him and held out her hand.

"Oh, Mrs."

"I shouldn't shake your hand, mine's so grubby, I don't want to get you covered in soot."

"Nonsense, I can easily wash it off. I am so happy to meet you at last."

He was fascinated by her American accent.

Melissa was usually upstairs, but today they had decided to have afternoon tea in the garden, to enjoy a bit of fresh air, before they set off later, for another evening in the smoky jazz club. Matty had proved to be a great hit with his saxophone.

Blackie thought Melissa was charming.

She asked him about his family, how long he had been a coalman, did he hate the messy work, were his customers nice to him?

He knew a bit about her of course. He delivered to all the Mansion flats in the block and some of her neighbours had been only too keen to share the news of the young rich widow and her two Black companions.

He liked the way she was so natural with Ruth and Matty. She treated them just like friends, equals even, although it was obvious she was the one with the money.

"My wife is called Daisy and we have one daughter, Florence. She has left school now."

"She didn't like it much. Once she had learnt to read and write, she couldn't see much point in it. We were a bit worried how she was going to earn a living, but now she seems to have taken a fancy to sewing. And is pretty good at it."

Daisy put down her teacup and glanced over at Ruth. Ruth knew exactly what she was thinking and nodded her head.

"We have been thinking about getting someone to help make our dresses. Ruth does a great job, but now she is married to a famous musician, she doesn't have as much time."

They all smiled at her reference to Matty being famous.

"Do you think your daughter might like to come and help us? Maybe three days a week?"

"Perhaps you would all like to come for afternoon tea on Sunday and we can discuss it?"

Frederick insisted on taking them in the car.

"It will be a little outing for Fred and I. We don't often get to that part of town."

So they had arrived in Bloomsbury in style, in the grey Rolls Royce, and as they stepped out of the car, Flo was sure she could see some of the curtains twitching in the mansion block.

"Bet none of those people realise you're usually their coalman, Dad."

Because they were used to the splendour of Fredericks house in Marylebone, none of them felt in the least uncomfortable in Melissa's grand home. They were used to beautiful antique furniture, old Persian rugs, expensive art and silk and satin drapes.

But neither Daisy, Flo or Blackie, had ever spent any time in the company of black people. Blackie had of course met both Ruth and Matty, when he delivered their coal, but the other day when he had sat in the garden, was the first time he had really engaged in any conversation with them.

"They seem like very nice people, both the lady of the house, Mrs. Cummings, and her two friends. I think you'll like them."

He had been telling Daisy and Flo about the invitation to visit on Sunday.

He paused, not sure exactly what to say next.

"They come from Alabama in the Deep South of America. She's a young widow and they are her friends from home. Very good looking married couple. He plays the saxophone in a jazz band. She's a dressmaker. Oh and they're black."

"Oh my, you are so beautiful."

Flo was looking directly at Ruth as she spoke.

"And your husband is so handsome."

"Do you really play in a jazz band?"

"Are all the other band members as black as you?"

Matty laughed, a deep throaty laugh.

"Yes, my dear, they are all black like me. Apparently the colour of our skin makes us very good musicians."

The afternoon went splendidly. Everyone was very relaxed, even when Flo said,

"Is it true that people in America are cruel to Black people, even though they're not slaves anymore and should be equal?"

Melissa swallowed hard before she replied.

How her Theo would have loved this feisty girl.

"Yes, my dear, I'm afraid it is rather true. I grew up on a cotton plantation and my parents weren't very nice to their black servants."

"But they weren't really bad people. They just copied the way their parents and grandparents had acted before them."

"If you are born into that life, you often have a sense of superiority and entitlement."

"But I firmly believe we are all equal, all God's children, whatever our colour."

"No matter if we are rich or poor, we should treat everyone as we would like to be treated."

By the time they left that afternoon, a deep bond had already been formed.

Between the rich young widow from the plantation, who had never wanted for anything in her entire life and the young girl, whose great-grandmother had died in the Workhouse.

Frederick insisted that young Fred drive Flo to Bloomsbury, every Tuesday, Thursday and Friday.

Mostly the three women just stayed at home, creating fabulous new dresses, but sometimes Melissa would get bored and decide it was time for an outing.

They went to all the fashion shows of course, to get inspiration and then trawled the shops for suitable fabrics. It was a very happy time for them all. Flo loved the enthusiasm the older women showed for her designs and she thoroughly enjoyed their company.

"Mrs Cummings has asked me to call her Melissa, Mum. She says it makes her feel like an old lady otherwise."

"She and Ruth are such lovely people, Mum. They don't have any airs and graces and don't treat me like I'm just the coalman's daughter."

"When I grow up, I want to be a lady just like them, kind and generous to everybody."

Daisy smiled.

Of course she was biased, but she thought they were very lucky to have her girl to help them. She was the kindest, sweetest girl you could ever meet. No wonder everybody loved her.

Flo had grown into a magnificent young woman. She was tall, even taller than her father and she had such a good, caring heart. She rarely saw the bad in anybody. It helped of course that she had grown up surrounded by love. So many people loved her, everyone at the Marylebone house of course and now it seemed her new employers did too.

Daisy just hoped that one day her girl would find a good man. A man who would cherish and look after her.

LONDON
1923

Flo had been working at Melissa's for a whole year now. She was so happy with her life.

She moved between the Mews Cottage, Frederick's mansion in Marylebone, and Melissa's place in Bloomsbury with ease. She was loved and welcomed in all three places.

It was summer now and although Fred still drove her to Bloomsbury every morning, she had persuaded her parents to let her get the omnibus home in the afternoons.

Daisy had a morbid fear of omnibuses, after her foster mother Maisy had thrown herself under one all those years ago.

"Come on my love."

"Our girl is growing up and we should give her a bit of freedom. She'll be fine. The journey will only take about half an hour and we can get Matty or Ruth to see her to the bus stop if you're worried. And she'll get off just round the corner from here, so she'll be quite safe."

Blackie hated the thought of his precious daughter roaming the streets of London too, but he knew they had to allow it.

Flo had no idea how magnificent she was. She was head and shoulders taller than most of the other girls who got on the bus every afternoon. And so she was noticed.

"Mum, I've met someone."

"Oh have you love?"

Daisy was busy laying the table for dinner. She always liked it to be ready for when Blackie walked in the door.

"Yes and I really like him."

Daisy stopped laying out the cutlery and looked up.

"Oh love. Well, I guess you'd better tell me before your Dad comes in."

She was only too aware of how her husband would react, if he thought young men were sniffing around his precious girl.

"I met him on the bus Mum."

"He works at the Docks and he lives in Southwark. His name is Joe. Joe Smith. He's a bit older than me, but he's really nice Mum, I really like him."

Daisy suddenly felt as though there was lead in her heart.

A Docker!

She had always hoped for a good marriage for her girl. It was very unlikely a Docker from Southwark would be a suitable husband. She remembered old John, her foster father from the slums. He had been a docker. A pleasant enough man, but rather uncouth and much too fond of beer.

"What docks does he work at?"

Perhaps she could get Blackie to make some enquiries about the lad. After he had calmed down, of course.

"Surrey Commercial Docks, south of the river. Quite near his home I think."

Her voice sounded calmer than she felt as she replied. "Where does he live exactly?"

"Peabody Buildings, Southwark Street. He lives with his Dad and two brothers. They all work on the docks too. And his sister and her family live next door. There were two more brothers but one died in the war and the other one died just after he was born. His mum died too."

Daisy could hear the catch in her voice. Her soft hearted girl was already worrying about this man's dead mother!"

"And do you know him well, love?"

"Oh yes, we've been sitting together at the bus stop for a few weeks now."

"Why is he at your bus stop, when he lives the other way, over the river?"

She was aware that she was asking too many questions, but wanted to have as much information to present to Blackie as possible.

"Oh he's been working over this side for a few months, at St. Katherine's Docks."

"Anyway Mum, I asked him to come here for tea on Sunday, I hope that's alright?"

Blackie was amazingly calm about it.

"Look love. You married a coalman, some people think a docker is a step above that."

"We must give the lad a chance, but I will ask around. I know quite a few blokes who work at St. Katherine's, they'll tell me if he's a wrong un."

The two Freds and Sybil were also invited for tea.

Poor Joe was bombarded with questions, interrogated even, from the moment he arrived in the Mews house, until the moment he left.

"I'm so sorry Joe. My family were very rude and nosy. I'm sorry if they upset you."

She sounded tearful.

He stopped suddenly, turned round and swept her into his arms.

He was a big man, a good six inches taller than her and very strong from lifting at the docks all day.

"If you think that was hard Flo, you wait till you meet my lot. But we mustn't let any of them change our minds. I love you and I want to marry you."

She was shocked. She knew he liked her, but this was the first time he had mentioned love or marriage.

She suddenly felt very shy and wriggled in his arms.

"Do you mean that Joe? Do you really want to marry me?"

The following Sunday they all went to Southwark.

In Fredericks Rolls Royce.

Joe was waiting in the street for them and whistled when he saw the car.

"Oh my, I'd never have been brave enough to talk to you if I'd known about your posh relatives."

Old Frederick laid his hand gently on Joe's arm.

"My dear boy, having a smart car, or a bit of money, doesn't make you a better man."

"It just means you were lucky enough to be born into a wealthy family".

"How you live your life and treat other people, is what counts."

It was a very happy afternoon.

Joe's family were very welcoming and were obviously delighted that he had met and fallen in love with such a nice girl. Okay, so he was a bit older, six years to be precise, but that meant he earned a bit more than a younger lad and could afford to look after a wife.

They could all see that the young couple were mad about each other. In a calm, quiet kind of way.

Flo was only 17, so it was agreed that they could get engaged straightaway, but wait another year before they married.

Daisy rather hoped it would all fade away, but she was wrong.

Flo had found her soulmate, without even looking.

They were married on Christmas Eve 1924 at the Parish Church of St. Saviour with St. Peter in Southwark. It started snowing gently as they came out of the church.

Daisy stood with Blackie, looking at their girl as she posed on the church steps, with her new husband. She had tears in her eyes.

"Oh Daisy, don't go crying again. She'll be alright, he's a good man."

Sybil spoke quietly and they all nodded in agreement. They had all become quite fond of Joe.

Daisy looked around her, all the people she loved most in the world were here.

There were the two Freds, both looking mature and dignified these days, more comfortable in their own skins.

Then there was Sybil, who had always been more like a mother to her and a loving Grandma to Flo.

And of course her beloved Blackie.

Standing just to one side, but very much part of their family group, were Melissa, Ruth and Matty.

"What a very mixed bunch we are," Daisy thought to herself. "But there is so much love between us. It just proves that it doesn't matter where you come from, whether you are rich or poor, Black or White, or like men better than women, we are all the same underneath and sometimes you are lucky enough to find each other and make a family."

At that very moment, Flo looked across at them and waved.

She looked absolutely stunning and so very happy.

She had made herself the most beautiful wedding gown of thick white satin and over the top she wore a long, white velvet cloak, with a hood trimmed with white fur.

A few snowflakes fell on her face and they watched as her new husband gently brushed them off.

"Don't you worry my love, she's going to be just fine. My boy adores her, worships the ground she walks on"

Joe's father spoke gruffly.

"I think we should all get on to the reception now, before we freeze to death."

ARTILLERY PASSAGE
SPITALFIELDS, LONDON
1930

There had been a lot of discussion as to where Florence and Joe would live after the wedding.

He had been quite keen for them to live with his father and brothers in Southwark, but she was determined to stay north of the river.

"It does make sense love. When we have babies, there's no-one to help me at your place, but if we are over this way, there is Mum, Sybil, Ruth and Melissa. I won't ever have to try and cope on my own."

There was no way he could refuse her, his beautiful new bride.

He still couldn't believe his luck.

All his mates down the docks teased him about his posh, fancy wife.

But there was no malice in their teasing.

They had all met Flo at the wedding and she had charmed them with her natural easy manner. In fact, some of them were now half in love with her themselves.

"Well, rents are a bit more expensive here love, I'm not sure what we could afford?"

After their honeymoon they had come back to the Mews House, to stay with her Mum and Dad while they looked for a place of their own.

Florence had already made up her mind exactly where she wanted them to live.

Now she just had to convince him.

"Well, I thought if you got a job permanently at St. Katherine's Docks, we should live somewhere nearby, so you can just walk to work every day."

She paused, letting that thought sink in.

"Oh love, some of those areas round the docks are a bit rough."

She had expected this reaction and had all her answers ready.

"I know, but there are some nice bits too. For example round Shoreditch and Spitalfields, they've done lots of work to make it better. Lots of the slums have gone."

"Oh Flo, not Shoreditch. I'd always be worried about another Ripper."

He was referring, of course, to the Jack the Ripper murders that had taken place in the East End almost 40 years previously.

She knew this was a hard one to argue.

Some of the lanes and alleyways around there were still a bit dark and gloomy.

But Flo, at almost 6 feet tall, was like a magnificent female warrior, a Boudica of the 20th century, and she had no intention of letting a long dead maniac interfere with her plans.

"Well actually Joe, I've already found the perfect place."

He groaned.

He had only been married to this young woman for a few weeks, but he already knew that once she had made up her mind, it was impossible to budge her.

"Oh Flo, don't you think we should have discussed all this first, before you went off gallivanting round the East End?"

But he knew his objections were useless.

If he had his way, they would have been settled in Southwark by now, in the flat in Peabody Buildings where he had grown up. He would know everyone around him and have a pint with his mates after work every Friday before going home to his nice little wife and a hot dinner.

He smiled to himself at the irony of it.

When had he, the big, strapping lad from the docks, started taking orders from a bossy young woman?

He looked at her across the table. She had insisted on having this conversation the minute he got in from work. He realised now that it had been an ambush, to catch him when he was tired and hungry. She had sent her mum and dad next door to see Sybil and Fred, so they would be alone.

"I think you'll love it, Joe. Shall I tell you all about it now, then perhaps we could go and see it together on Saturday?"

Saturday turned out to be a dull and rainy day. The kind of day when most of the city looked grey and uninviting.

He was still reeling from their conversation the other evening. He couldn't believe what Flo was planning. He had thought getting married just meant having someone there to keep his home warm, clean, and cosy, to always have a hot meal on the table, and to produce a few babies. How wrong he had been; his Flo had much bigger ideas.

The house they had come to see was on Artillery Passage in Spitalfields.

A five-storey Georgian house with a courtyard garden and huge cellar.

It was in a row of similar houses, all fronting directly onto the narrow, cobbled thoroughfare.

"What do you think? Isn't it just perfect?"

Joe was speechless for a few moments.

"Oh Flo, do you really think this is a good idea?"

"Yes, I really do. I'm so excited Joe, please say you're happy too."

The house was just a ten minute walk to the docks, there was a pub on the corner, and the neighbours seemed quite respectable, so he couldn't think of any real objections to her plan.

They could never have afforded it on their own, but Old Frederick had stepped in. Flo had confided her plan to the old man before she mentioned it to Joe.

Joe was still unsure.

"Are you really sure, Flo? Do you really think you can do this? We don't want to waste the old man's money?"

He was very worried when she told him what she intended to do.

Thanks to Frederick Palmer's generosity, the couple was able to buy the house on Artillery Passage.

"I absolutely insist. You are like a granddaughter to me. I was going to leave you some money in my will, but I would much rather give it to you now to help you when you most need it. My only stipulation is that it is owned in your name only; do you think Joe will mind that?"

"Why do you want to do that? Shouldn't it be in both our names if we're married?"

"My dear girl. It would just make me feel happier knowing you had something of your own. Joe will obviously pay all the bills and support you but this will make it easier for him too, as he won't have to worry about paying rent."

And so they moved to the big house on Artillery Passage and Flo fulfilled her dream.

Not just the dream of a happy marriage in a beautiful new home.

Her dream was to open a dress shop, and her new house had a glass shop front, perfect for her plan.

Just three weeks after moving in, she held a grand opening.

Daisy stood on the cobbled pavement outside and looked through the shop window.

Inside she could see her daughter, her beloved Flo, holding hands with her handsome husband. Several smartly dressed ladies were flicking through the dresses hanging on the wooden rails. She spotted Ruth and Melissa talking animatedly while sipping champagne.

Blackie leant down and gently wiped away the tears that were streaming down her face.

"Oh Blackie, I had no idea she was going to call it that."

He looked at the huge, gold lettering etched on the glass of the window.

"POLLY'S"

"Thank you all for coming tonight. I am so thrilled to welcome you to my little shop. Please feel free to try anything on. If you don't like anything already here, I can create another design for you.

I would like to thank my husband, Joe, for all his hard work helping me to get the shop ready in time. And my mum and dad, Sybil, Frederick and Fred, for their constant encouragement."

She looked across at Frederick as she said this.

She had wanted to mention his generosity, after all, none of this would have been possible without it, but she knew he would have hated being singled out and praised. Despite his wealth and social standing, he was actually a quiet, rather shy man.

"But most of all, I would like to thank Polly, my grandmother, who died before I was born. She was a great dressmaker, and that is why I have called my shop after her."

The shop proved to be a great success.

Melissa insisted that all her Bloomsbury friends visited, and Frederick ensured that everyone he knew from the arts and antiques world knew of its existence.

Because Flo's designs were so unique, her clients could be confident that they would never see another society woman wearing the same outfit. She became the talk of the town.

Of course, most of her neighbours in Artillery Passage were too poor to afford one of her beautiful creations, and she often saw them peering longingly through the windows.

Flo only ever had two or three items on display in her shop window, and one of them was always the first dress she had ever made. It was the one with fabric hanging like petals, the one that had started her on this journey.

If she heard of a young girl in the neighbourhood who was getting married, she always offered to make her wedding dress free of charge, so long as she paid for the fabrics.

Fabric, even quality fabric that for one reason or another never quite made it to the big flashy department stores, could be bought quite cheaply in the street markets. Sometimes it was just excess stock that a manufacturer was desperate to shift, or perhaps it had slight flaws in the weave. Usually, it was good enough quality for a fraction of the price one would pay in the West End. Flo bought a lot of fabrics from the markets for her own creations, and all the stallholders liked her. She was feisty and always tried to get a bargain, but she was also kind and caring, asking them about their families.

Flo gave birth to her and Joe's first son, Benjamin, in late 1925, almost a year after their wedding.

There was great rejoicing.

All the families came for the christening, and Flo smiled as she looked at the little group cooing over the baby.

Daisy was holding him, every inch the proud grandmother, while Blackie was standing right beside her, ready to catch the precious bundle if necessary.

Melissa, Ruth, and Sybil, all wearing velvet flowery dresses that Flo had made them especially for the occasion, hovered nearby, waiting their turn for a cuddle.

The two Freds, Joe, Matty, and Joe's father and brothers were all deep in conversation about motor cars. Old Fred had his Rolls-Royce of course, and Melissa had just bought a Ford Model T.

In 1927, their second son, John Joseph, was born.

Both the boys thrived and Flo and Joe were delighted with their little family. The shop was doing quite well, although Joe did worry about Flo staying up all hours sewing and then having to get up early to look after the children while he went off to work.

"You could give it up, you know, love. Now you've got the boys to look after. We could turn the shop into a nice little parlour."

Flo rarely lost her temper, particularly with her husband.

"How dare you, how dare you even suggest such a thing? It would break my heart to shut the shop. You know how much I love it. And I don't neglect the boys, you know I don't."

It was true. She was a wonderful mother.

It was a dark and wintry day when Benjamin first became sick.

At first he just had a sore throat. Then it developed into a barking cough.

Frederick sent the best London doctors to the house, but it was too late. Their precious little boy died, at just two years old, of the dreaded diphtheria.

They were all worried that Flo would never recover.

She was absolutely beside herself at losing her beautiful boy.

Not even Baby John could distract her from her dark thoughts.

Daisy was very anxious.

She and Blackie had moved into the house on Artillery Passage to help Flo and Joe cope with everything.

They had closed up the shop and hung a big black wreath made from satin ribbon in the window.

"Oh Blackie, whatever can we do to help her?"

"I remember how awful it was when our babies died. I just wanted to jump in the grave with them. I'm so worried about what she might do."

As well as losing two babies herself, Daisy remembered when she had been just a young girl living in the slums, and her foster mother Maisy had lost a child.

Maisy had been so sad that she had almost lost her mind at the time, and she had later taken her own life by jumping in front of the bus.

A month after they had buried Benjamin in a tiny white coffin that haunted Daisy in her dreams, they woke early, just after dawn, to the sound of movement from downstairs.

Creeping down the creaky, wooden steps with a stick in his hand, ready to fight off any intruders, Blackie was amazed to see his daughter Flo. She was sitting on the shop floor, sorting through piles of fabric.

"Oh hello, Dad. Did I wake you? I'm so sorry. I couldn't sleep, so I thought I'd get the shop ready to open tomorrow."

She was very pale, with black circles under her eyes.

"Oh love, do you think that's a good idea? Perhaps you should take a bit more time off."

"Taking more time isn't going to bring him back, so what's the point?"

Her voice was dull, she sounded as though all her life and energy had died with her baby.

Blackie walked over and enfolded her in his big, strong arms, and she put out a small wail.

"Oh Dad, how on earth am I ever going to get through this?"

He held her tightly and stroked her hair, just like he used to when she was a little girl.

Daisy came down the stairs a few minutes later and found her husband and daughter both sobbing. She hugged them both tightly, and for a long time they stayed right there, embracing on the shop floor.

Then she told Flo how she had felt exactly the same both times she had lost her baby boys.

"Oh my love, it's the worst thing in the world to lose a child. Especially one you've loved and looked after, one who has started to become his own person. I can't pretend you'll ever get over it. Time will help, but the pain and sadness will always be with you. You just get used to it."

Flo had never heard her mother talk like this before. She had only been young when both her brothers were stillborn.

"Oh Mum, will I ever feel happy again?" She felt as though her heart had been snapped in two.

"I know I still have my little John, so I am lucky, but now I'm always worried about losing him too. I just thought if I opened the shop, it might take my mind off things a bit."

And so she did open the shop the very next day, and all her customers came flooding back.

Daisy and Blackie stayed on for another couple of months, until they knew she was over the worst. They were wonderful grandparents, so Joe could go off to work every day knowing his wife and baby were in good hands.

He had been so worried about his girl. At one stage, he had thought that her overwhelming sadness might cause her to lose her sanity. He had never seen such raw grief before, and it really frightened him.

Flo had been in the early stages of her third pregnancy when little Benjamin died.

For months afterwards, she had not eaten or slept properly, and they had all been convinced she would lose the baby.

To everyone's great joy, little Violet Frederika Smith made her safe entrance into the world on a bright summer day in 1930.

Flo started smiling again.

LONDON
1947

They had all survived the dreadful war years from 1939 to 1945, although many of their friends and neighbours had lost husbands and sons. Killed in action in far off lands.

Others had come home badly wounded, both in body and mind.

Flo was so grateful that her Joe had been in a reserved occupation as a docker, otherwise she would probably have lost him, too. John had still been at school, too young to be called up when the war started. Although he had been desperate to become a soldier and go off with his mates to fight for King and Country, he was just 16 when the war ended, so he never got the chance.

Flo looked around the table at her little family.

It was a Sunday afternoon and they were all at her house, celebrating Violet's 17th birthday.

Violet was now a beautiful young woman.

Fred looked as dapper as always, although there was a sadness about him nowadays.

His master and best friend, Frederick Palmer, had died a year ago at the ripe old age of 98.

They had been together for so many years that now there was a huge void in his life.

Fred was no spring chicken himself having just celebrated his 86th birthday, but he was still fit and healthy.

Sitting next to him was Sybil. She was 83 now, but also seemed younger than her years.

A few years before he died, Old Frederick had established a home for retired gentlemen in his grand house in Marylebone.

He and Fred had enjoyed setting it up, attracting like-minded men who had become impoverished in their old age but were now thrilled to find themselves living out their last years in such splendid surroundings. It was a hugely expensive project, but a lack of money had never been a problem for Frederick.

"Now you two," he had asked Fred and Sybil to come to his bedroom.

Lately he had been spending more and more time unable to get out of bed.

"You know how much you both mean to me. You've been my family for the last 50 or so years, and I really don't know how I could have done it without you both. Now, now don't cry. We all have to be strong and sensible about this. I can't go on forever. Let's face it, neither of you are getting any younger either, and I want to make sure you will be alright when I'm gone. I've already given Daisy the Mews Cottage and Flo has her shop and house on Artillery Passage. I have made bequests to help Vi and young John get established. I know you will both probably want to stay here, but I also want you to have somewhere to run away to, when you need a change. So I've signed over the Brighton house into both your names."

The Brighton house was an elegant Regency townhouse in the Royal Crescent, right on the seafront. Brighton in East Sussex was just an hour's car journey from London, and easily reached by train. It had become a great favourite escape of the two men over the years and after Frederick bought the house, they had stayed there most weekends. The seaside town with its bracing promenade strolls, two piers (the West Pier and the Palace Pier), and the Royal Pavilion, had more than enough to keep the two men occupied.

Since Old Frederick's death, Brighton had become a bit of a haven for his two friends.

Every time they felt their sadness beginning to overwhelm them, they got in the car and drove straight down to Brighton. Fred was still a good driver, although he had to wear glasses now. Ten years previously, the Rolls-Royce had been exchanged for a Jaguar Roadster SS100, a beautiful cream-coloured car with red leather upholstery. It had been Old Frederick's pride and joy.

They hadn't had the heart to part with it after he died, but most of the time it just sat idle in the Mews garage.

These days, they usually went to Brighton along with Daisy and Blackie.

Sometimes Flo, Joe, and the children would go too, but of course Vi and John were getting a bit too grown up to want to go on weekend outings with the old ones. They would much rather hang about with their young friends.

John had recently turned 18, just a year older than his sister. He was a rather quiet and serious boy. His dad had gotten him a job in the offices down at St. Katherine's Docks, but he had bigger ambitions. He wanted to be an engineer. With the money Old Fred had left him, he was going to evening classes at the local technical college and then planned to go on to university.

Flo looked across the table at her mum and dad.

How she loved them. They had been her rock through that awful time when Benjamin died. Daisy was still beautiful at 60 years old. Her hair was grey now instead of blonde, and she usually wore it piled up in a loose coil on the top of her head.

Blackie was still handsome, although he now walked with a slight stoop, a legacy from all the years of lugging heavy sacks of coal. He was retired now and instead of the horse and cart, he drove an Austin A40, which he had bought with his bequest from the old man. Frederick had ensured that everyone received a share of his estate, and had always been impressed with the way Blackie had loved and taken care of Daisy for so many years.

Ruth and Matty were there too, both now in their sixties but seemingly ever youthful. Ruth often helped Flo out in her shop, especially when she had too many orders to cope with all the sewing herself.

Matty was still in demand at the jazz club. He played the saxophone like a dream now.

And Melissa.

Flo looked across at her friend and smiled.

There was only a six-year difference in their ages, and they had become the greatest of friends over the years. Flo was now 41 and felt that every one of those years showed on her face, but Melissa was still extraordinarily lovely. The years hardly seemed to have changed her at all.

Melissa had never re-married. She had had plenty of offers of course, but no one could ever match up to her Theo. He was her soulmate, the man she had married at just 19 back in Alabama, who had died just a year later, breaking her heart. Though she missed him dearly still, she had made the very most of her life without him. She had travelled with Ruth and Matty to England for a single holiday so long ago, a year after Theo died, and had made a new life for herself in London. She had only been back to America once, very briefly, to attend her grandfather's funeral in 1927.

Her conservative Southern relatives had been shocked at her appearance.

They were not used to the London fashions — the short hair, the looser, shorter clothing, not a bodice in sight. And she smoked now, balancing a silver cigarette holder in one gloved hand whilst sipping from a martini glass in the other. Of course they had still been in the time of Prohibition in America, but her daddy always made sure he had a full liquor cabinet.

Matty and Ruth had travelled with Melissa, and though they were both delighted to be reunited with their relatives, it had saddened them hugely to compare their comfortable London lives with those of their families still working on the plantations.

Matty's grandfather, Old Freddie, and Bess, the only original slaves still on the property, had both died during their long absence.

Matty was glad. The old pair had suffered so much during their lifetimes, and now they were at peace. At least his grandfather had known of his new life, his happiness with Ruth, his success with the saxophone. He had written to the old man every week, for the whole six years he had been away.

Pearl, Bess's granddaughter, presented Matty with the letters, hundreds of them that Old Freddie had stored in an old wooden box.

"These were your granddaddy's most treasured possessions. Every afternoon, he and my grandma would sit under the old tree and read them. Time and time over."

Matty cried then, for a long, long time, mourning the old man and the sad life he had been forced to lead. Just because of the "accident" of birth.

The first time he had met Frederick Palmer, the truth of that statement had really hit him. An accident of birth. His old granddaddy and the rich man from London had shared the same name, but their lives had been so vastly different. All because of an accident of birth.

Even as a young man, he had agreed with Theo and Melissa's viewpoint.

A view she still expressed at every opportunity, hoping to persuade less-informed souls.

"Just because you are born into a life of poverty, or your skin is black, doesn't make you a lesser person. Some of the best and smartest people I have ever met never got the chance to be their true selves, to fulfill all their capabilities and ambitions, just because of the life they were born into."

None of them could wait to leave America. It had been good to see everyone, but they realised their real home was in London now.

Melissa had spoken to her father during the visit and he had agreed, in light of her refusal to return to Alabama, to buy back the old house she and Theo had lived in on the plantation. This would give her enough capital to buy the London mansion flat.

He had been paying the rent on it anyway.

Flo continued looking at her family, seated around her kitchen table.

Apart from the awful war years, life had been pretty kind to them all. Of course, they had had the normal ups and downs that come with being human — death, sickness, love, and loss. But they also had each other and that had proved to be worth much more than anything.

"Do you think I could open my presents now?

They all looked at Vi and smiled. She had never lost her sense of joy and excitement.

As a little girl she had loved birthdays, and it seemed that even now, when she was almost grown up, with a job and a young man, nothing would dull her joy.

Her young man, Bert, chuckled.

"Oh Vi, you're so funny. Maybe none of us have even bought you presents."

He spoke with great affection. They had been courting for almost a year now and he was madly in love with her.

His full name was Albert Edward Smith, but everyone called him Bert.

He was the son of a distant cousin of her dad's, and Vi had met him at a Christmas party at her grandad's house in Southwark. He was five years older than she and very charming. Bert was a docker of course, as most of her father's family members were, but he was well-read and very interested in the world around him. He had spent hours talking to Matty and Ruth about their lives on the plantation and loved to hear Blackie's stories of his life as a coalman, trudging around the city with his horse and cart.

All the family liked him, but they thought Vi was still far too young to settle down.

Vi had left school at 15.

She hated sewing, so there was no way she wanted to inherit the shop.

She did love serving the customers, but her ambitions went way beyond Artillery Passage.

Without mentioning it to anyone, she had managed to talk her way into getting a little Saturday job at one of the posh West End department stores after leaving school.

She had only just passed her 15th birthday at the time, but she soon impressed the shop managers with her dedication, good manners, and excellent customer service skills. In no time at all she was offered a full time position and now, just two years on, she was second in charge of ladies knitwear. One day, she intended to be in charge of an entire department.

It was just a few months after her 17th birthday party.

"Mum, I've got something to tell you."

Flo looked up from her sewing.

"Oh hello, love. I didn't hear you come in. You've finished early tonight?"

Usually Vi was the last one home from work.

She often stayed late to help the window dressers, handing them stock or pins or props, while they created glorious window displays. She was ambitious and believed that if only she could get the chance to dress a window, she too could do a splendid job. Sometimes, on the bus coming home, she was so engrossed in her daydreams that she missed her stop and had to walk an extra ten minutes back to Artillery Passage.

"Mum, can you stop sewing a minute? This is important."

Flo realised from the tone of her voice that she was upset. Vi was rarely anything but happy. She had been a sunny, contented little girl and was no different now that she was fully grown.

Before she could get the words out, Vi burst into tears. Flo leapt up from the table and hugged her daughter tightly.

"Oh love, what on earth's wrong?"

"I'm going to have a baby."

Flo felt as though the bottom had dropped out of her world. Of course, these accidents happened all the time. But not to her girl. Surely not to her lovely girl.

"Oh love,"

"How are we ever going to tell Dad? He'll be so upset and disappointed with me."

She sounded so forlorn.

Joe was furious of course, but not with his girl.

"Right, I'm off to Southwark right now to sort out that bastard. How dare he get my girl in the family way?"

"Oh Joe, don't be hasty. He's a nice lad, and it wasn't just him who got them into this mess."

"Please, Dad. Don't. He loves me, I know he does, and we were talking about getting married next year. As soon as you let us. I just wish we'd run off to Gretna Green now, like Bert wanted."

Her parents were shocked. They thought they knew everything about their daughter, but obviously there was a lot she never told them.

"Anyway, he doesn't even know about the baby yet."

"You haven't told him?" Joe was incredulous.

"No Dad, I only just found out for sure today, and I didn't want to worry him until I had to."

Her words trailed off and turned into a loud sob.

The next evening Bert turned up at the house on Artillery Passage as usual.

He came for his dinner after work every Tuesday, Thursday, and Saturday.

He had no idea of the drama awaiting him.

Flo and Joe stayed discreetly upstairs while the young couple talked in the kitchen.

They heard muffled voices and occasional sobbing. Joe was desperate to go down and intervene, but she stopped him.

"No love, we must let them try and sort this out themselves. She knows we're up here if she needs us."

Eventually they came upstairs, and Flo's heart went out to the young man.

He looked like a pale, frightened little boy instead of the big, strapping man he was.

"Mr. and Mrs. Smith, I'm so sorry. Please forgive me. I love Vi and would never hurt her."

"I just feel so embarrassed."

"And angry with myself."

"I should have behaved like a gentleman."

"Until we were married. And I do want to marry her. As soon as possible."

"That's all I've ever wanted. To marry her."

Vi refused to wear a white dress. Although her bump wasn't really showing, it turned out she was already five months pregnant.

"It's no good Mum, I just wouldn't feel right wearing virginal white when everyone knows I'm not."

Flo was very upset. She had spent years dreaming of sewing a beautiful wedding dress for her only daughter.

"I thought you could make me a nice yellow suit instead, perhaps with a matching hat."

Yellow had always been Vi's favourite colour, even as a little girl.

Probably because it suited her sunny nature.

So they tracked down the most beautiful sunshine-yellow silk fabric, and in just five days Flo had made the perfect outfit. It showed off Vi's lovely figure, but had a little extra material cleverly sewn down the front to hide her growing tummy. The matching hat was perfect, a cloche style made of yellow felt, with a large silk bow to match the suit.

"Oh Mum, thank you. I look like a film star."

Blackie, Joe, Fred, and Matty had taken Bert out for a drink the night before the wedding and had read him the riot act.

"If you ever do anything, and I mean anything, to hurt my girl or make her sad, I will find you and I will kill you."

"Now, now, Joe." Blackie spoke quietly.

"What Joe means, Bert, is that Vi is very, very precious to all of us, and it's very important that you take care of her and treat her like a princess. And the baby too, when it comes."

"You have my word that no harm will ever come to her. I love her very much and I'm going to do my best to be a good husband."

The young man spoke with such sincerity that all of them felt a little guilty for doubting him.

"Well, just mind you do. I shall be keeping a beady eye on you, my lad. Now let's have another pint, before we get you home."

Everyone showed up to their beautiful wedding, of course.

Fred and Sybil were both thinking how much Vi looked like their beloved Polly. At least she was getting married to a good, decent man.

Their Polly had been so poorly treated, repeatedly raped by their master, which resulted in Daisy, then dying in agony trying to give birth to another bastard child of his. At least their darling Vi would never have to suffer like that.

Vi's grandparents, Daisy and Blackie, watched as she spoke her vows in a clear, loud voice.

Their bride looked stunning in her yellow attire.

Melissa had insisted on paying for her wedding bouquet, which was exquisite.

It was huge, made of yellow roses, white orchids, and trailing ivy.

"Oh Mum, it's so beautiful." Vi had burst into tears when it was delivered.

"It's just like the one Princess Elizabeth had at her wedding."

And indeed it was.

Melissa had found out who designed the royal bouquet and asked them to make a similar one for her young friend. Constance Spry, the celebrated florist, had overseen it herself.

Fred and Sybil had insisted that Vi and Bert use the Brighton house for their honeymoon and Blackie and Daisy drove them there. A group of young people (Bert's friends from the docks and the girls Vi worked with in town) had tied old tin cans and horseshoes to the car bumper, so they left the wedding reception in a flurry of excitement and noise.

Vi was glad her grandparents were in the car with them. She suddenly felt very young and rather shy. She turned her head and found her new husband staring at her.

"Oh Vi, you look so beautiful. I reckon I'm the luckiest man alive."

By the time they returned three weeks later, they were both sunburnt and a little fatter.

"Oh Mum, you should have *seen* what we ate."

"Ice cream every day, sometimes twice a day. Fish and chips most days, and candy floss from the pier. Bert even made me try jellied eels and whelks, but I didn't like them much."

Flo was delighted to see her girl looking so well and happy.

Daisy had already told her how impressed she and Blackie had been to see the way Bert treated Vi. They all stayed together for the first few days in Brighton, just so Vi's grandparents could show the newlywed couple the ropes and introduce them to the housekeeper and cleaning lady of the house.

"He does love her, anyone can see that. Although he's so big and a bit rough around the edges, he really looks after her. I think it's going to be alright, love."

Daisy spoke gently to her daughter. She remembered only too well how fragile Flo had been after losing baby Benjamin. If anything happened to Vi, she wasn't sure Flo could cope.

But Vi flourished. She carried on working until the week before her baby was due.

She loved her job and was mortified at the thought of having to give it up to stay home and look after the newborn.

Vi and Bert had decided to stay in the house on Artillery Passage with her mum and dad for the first couple of months after the wedding. Then they were planning to move to Peabody Buildings in Southwark, so they could be nearer to Bert's work at the Surrey Commercial Docks.

His dad and both his brothers worked there too, so it seemed to make sense.

"I don't think our Vi's very keen to move to Southwark. It'll be hard for her to move in with strangers, especially when she's got a new baby. I wish they could just stay here, with us. We've got plenty of room."

Joe sighed. He had heard this so many times from his wife in the last few weeks.

"And I'm not sure how she'll handle it all, she's so young to be having a baby."

"Oh love, you were only young when you had Vi, and you coped."

"Yes, but that was different, Joe. I had Mum and Dad, and Sybil and Melissa and Ruth to help me. If she moves to Southwark, she'll have no one except Bert and his sister."

Flo had met Bert's sister on several occasions and wasn't sure she was quite their cup of tea. She was nice enough, but a bit common, and used bad language. And as for her children!

"Oh come on now, Flo, you're not being fair. Just because the girl is poor and lives in the buildings doesn't make her bad. Maybe if you were married to a brute who beat you and drank most of his wages in the pub every Friday night, maybe then you'd swear too."

"Oh and by the way, I grew up in Peabody Buildings too, and your family was decent enough to overlook that and treat me with respect."

Joe very rarely raised his voice or disagreed with his wife, but this conversation had struck a nerve.

He remembered how mortified he had been when they all turned up in Fred's Rolls-Royce to have tea with his family. He had always felt a bit of an outsider around Flo's family, even though they had all been really kind to him.

Being born poor was a scar that never faded.

Vi gave up work on a Friday afternoon and her friends threw a little farewell party for her at Lyons Corner House in Piccadilly.

She went into labour the following day, and baby Penelope was born just two hours later. The proud father came home from the docks laden down with celebration bottles of rum and boxes of cigars, gifts from his workmates, apparently.

"Oh Sybil, I'm really worried about our Vi. She doesn't stop crying and the baby doesn't seem to be thriving at all." Daisy sounded tearful.

Daisy had been spending a lot of time at Artillery Passage, helping her granddaughter with the new baby so that Flo could keep the shop open. The others had all been popping in on a regular basis. Sybil, Melissa, and Ruth were constant visitors.

Even the men — Fred, Matty, and of course the new great-grandad, Blackie — seemed unable to stay away. They fought over whose turn it was to hold the baby.

Everyone was worried about Vi.

She was certainly not coping. She loved her baby, there was no doubt about that. Even so, she certainly wasn't finding motherhood easy.

Some days she refused to get out of bed at all, just stayed under the covers with the baby in her cradle next to her.

And she cried.

Almost all of the time.

"I don't think it's just baby blues, Sybil. I remember what they're like, horrible for a while, but they soon pass. This is much worse than that."

Sybil hated seeing Daisy so upset. She had loved her since that awful day she was born in the slums of Stepney. And after her mum, Polly, had died, she and Fred had all but adopted her.

If only Old Frederick was still alive, he would have found some fancy doctor to help.

"Maybe we should ask Melissa if she knows anyone? I think some of her Bloomsbury friends are doctors. You know, the kind that specialise in troubles like these."

Of course it was still very taboo to talk about any kind of mental illness.

No one wanted to be carted off to the asylum, and many women still were, just for being unmarried mothers or for suffering any kind of depression.

It took Vi a whole year before she began to feel any better.

She knew how lucky she was to have such a strong, loving family around her; without them, she felt sure she would have completely lost her mind.

But sadly, she lost something else instead.

Bert, the big, strapping docker, could not cope with the sad, depressed person she had become. He missed his beautiful, charming, funny girl.

The baby cried all the time too, and as much as he loved them both, it wasn't enough.

He hated having to cross the river to go south every day to work, and resented the fact that Vi wouldn't move in with his father and brothers in Southwark.

He still went to the pub with his mates every Friday night after work, and of course there were plenty of young women there who were fancy-free and looking for a good time.

He stopped coming back to the house every night.

Then one day, he stopped coming back altogether.

It turned out that one of the girls from the pub was expecting a baby.

His baby.

And this girl was more than happy to live in Southwark with him.

Everyone thought that Vi would lose her mind when he left.

But instead, she flourished.

Now that there was no pressure on her to move away from her home, she relaxed and began to enjoy her baby. Bert had made it quite obvious that he wasn't interested in either of them; his focus was on his new girlfriend.

A few months after his departure, Vi realised she was pregnant again. It must have happened the last time, before he left for good.

She didn't tell anyone for several weeks. Somehow, if she didn't say the words aloud, they wouldn't be true.

"Mum, I've got something to tell you."

Flo looked up from feeding little Penny.

It hadn't taken long to shorten her name; everyone now called her Penny rather than Penelope. Some people just called her Pen.

"What?"

"I'm pregnant again."

Once they were over the shock, they rallied round her as she always knew they would. At least her babies would have this big and loving extended family, even though their own father didn't want them.

She had told Bert about the unplanned pregnancy too, of course.

Blackie, Joe, and Matty had all insisted on going down to Southwark with her.

Fred had wanted to go too, but they were all worried about him having a heart attack if he got too upset.

They were all quiet in the car going down.

The three men were remembering the night before the wedding, when they had taken young Bert out for a drink and threatened him with dire consequences if he ever hurt their girl.

"Oh Mum, it was so awful."

"Grandad and Matty had to drag Dad off of him. Bert looked really upset and a bit scared when we turned up. That floozy was there of course, in her tight, shiny little dress, with her big stomach. Bert's dad and brothers were nice though; his dad gave me a big hug when we left and said he was sorry and hoped I'd be alright. Bert couldn't even look at me, he obviously felt so guilty."

Even after everything that had happened, she still couldn't hate him.

Somehow, now that it was over and everything was said and done, she felt better.

She stroked her swelling tummy.

"You just stay all warm and cosy in there, little one. By the time you're ready to come, everything will all be alright."

When little Elizabeth Polly arrived in the world after a short and easy labour, it was to a very different household than the one her sister had been born into not so long before.

Fred had a weak heart now, so he and Sybil had recently moved into the Mews Cottage to live with Blackie and Daisy. All four of them had come to stay at Artillery Passage to help take care of Vi and the babies. Vi's older brother John had moved out; he was working up North and now only came home for holidays.

Melissa, Ruth, and Matty were regular visitors too. They were all very anxious about how Vi was going to cope this time around, especially with Bert out of the picture.

But they needn't have worried. Baby Elizabeth Polly's first months in the world were the opposite of her sister's.

She was a sunny, contented little girl, just like her mother had been.

HARLEM
1952

“I just ain’t sure this is a good idea, Samuel. Do we really have to?”

She knew it was a silly question. They were already on the ship, bound for England.

The *United States* was a splendid vessel.

According to her husband, it was “the fastest ocean liner ever built,” and they were now passengers on its maiden voyage.

She could still make out the tiny figures on the quayside, their friends who had come to see them off. In fact, it seemed to her that half the population of New York was at the docks today, watching the great liner depart. There were bands and ticker tape and hundreds of smiling faces.

“S’posing I never see these folks again. What if this ship sinks, like the *Titanic* did?”

The little boy standing next to her squeezed her hand.

“It’s okay Mum, Dad says it can’t sink. And it’s only going to take us four days to get there, so you can easily come back whenever you like.”

Jeremy was just five years old and very excited to be going on such a big adventure.

He had never been out of Harlem before, let alone crossed a big ocean and gone halfway around the world. But his dad had told him everything about this ship.

Samuel Davis was a 32-year-old man with big ambitions. He had been married to his wife, Winifred, for six years and he loved her and their son Jeremy with a passion.

But he didn't want their family to just exist, he wanted them to live a full, happy, and prosperous life.

He didn't believe they could do that if they stayed in Harlem.

He and Winifred had both descended from slaves.

Family history told tales of grinding poverty, cruel masters, escapes, lynchings, and finally "freedom." Samuel wasn't sure they could ever be considered truly free.

Growing up in Harlem in the 1930s and '40s was pretty grim for most people. Following the stock market crash of '29, there was little work, the unemployment rates were very high, and crime was a big problem.

Life was extreme in every way — good and bad — for a long time. Samuel was very bright and did well in school, but had to leave at 14 to help support his family. His ambition was to be an architect, but that quickly became out of the question for a relatively uneducated Black boy from the mean streets.

Instead, he took a job as a cleaner at Minton's Playhouse.

The Harlem nightclub, founded in 1938 by the saxophonist Henry Minton, was a wonderful place for a young man to work. The hours were often long and unsociable, but the atmosphere was electric. Some of the best jazz musicians played there. He met Dizzy Gillespie, Miles Davis, and Charlie Parker. They all took a liking to the quiet young cleaner and let him sit in on their practice sessions. Charlie even gave him an old saxophone and taught him how to play it.

December 7th, 1941, changed everything.

After the Pearl Harbor attack, young men from all over America, and of all skin colors, were drafted to go to war. Samuel was among them.

The Eighth Air Force unit arrived in England, on a base in East Anglia, and for the first time in his young life, Samuel was not treated like a second-class citizen.

Although most of the Black units were commanded by White officers, there was not the same kind of segregation in England as he had experienced back home.

Of course, race relations in wartime England were not perfect, but Samuel and his mates were warmly welcomed by the British public.

They were seen as rather exotic. They brought chewing gum, peanut butter, chocolate, and nylon stockings. They loved the Glenn Miller Orchestra and taught the local girls to jitterbug.

Sometimes, Samuel would even jump up on the stage and play his saxophone. Charlie Parker had taught him well.

He was tall, good-looking, and popular, and he often managed to trade a bar of chocolate or some nylon stockings for a quick kiss around the back of the dance hall.

Towards the end of the war in 1945, he decided that one day he would come back to England to settle and raise a family in this "green and pleasant land."

It wasn't an English girl who stole his heart, but the country itself.

Just a year after his return to the States, Samuel met Winifred.

His job at Minton's had changed; he was now a general assistant, helping the musicians to set up their gear and running errands for them. One day, he accompanied Dizzy to the Apollo Theatre, where he was doing a special one-night show.

"Hey boy, you can't go up on that stage. Only the performers are allowed up there."

He turned, ready to defend his position. Suddenly, he was tongue-tied.

The woman behind the words was the most lovely one he had ever seen. She was tall, with an hourglass figure squeezed into a pretty pink dress. Her hair looked natural, a mass of tight curls framing her beautiful black face.

They were married just two months later, and their son Jeremy was born exactly ten months after that.

Sometime later, Samuel had heard about the immigrants from the Caribbean — the ones who arrived in London in 1948 on the *Empire Windrush*.

He read England's Royal Commission on Population in 1949, which stated that "immigrants of good stock would be welcomed without reserve."

He tried very hard to persuade his wife to go, but she was stubborn.

"Oh baby, why can't you just be happy where we are? Life here ain't so bad."

The years ticked by as they always do, and although he was happy enough, Samuel constantly hankered after more. The couple had a nice apartment — well, one and a half rooms, with the other half a room acting as a combined kitchen and bathroom. Winifred always hung bright fabric on the windows and sewed matching cushions, but he was always aware that a beautiful creature like her deserved a much better environment in which to flourish.

One night Samuel came home from work and had hardly got in the door before he spoke. Winifred knew instantly that he was excited about something, just by the way his eyes were sparkling.

"We had a really interesting guy in the club today, Win. He was telling me about a new ship that's being built. Apparently it was designed by an American naval architect, William Gibbs, and it can be converted to a troopship or a hospital in wartime. It's mostly made of aluminium, nothing fancy or opulent like the old liners."

He paused, nothing.

"Wouldn't it be grand to go on the maiden voyage? I'm sure I could wangle us some cheap tickets."

Finally, "Where's it going, Sam?"

She knew the answer already, of course.

He had worked tirelessly to convince her. She was eventually beguiled by his stories of green fields, castles, and palaces. He promised her and their son a life of riches, of "more money and dignity than we could *ever* achieve here."

Winifred was a proud woman — a free woman — her freedom won on the blood and bones of her ancestors. Truth be told, she was extremely wary of moving her family across the world to a place where people with skin like hers, the colour of dark chocolate, would again be in the minority.

In the end Samuel won, and so here she was, leaving her home forever.

And sailing toward a foreign land she had never seen — one she did not particularly care to see at all.

On the bright side though, she had the two loves of her life with her, and she was determined to make the best of it.

SOUTH LONDON
1959

"I just wish it wasn't always so grey. Grey skies can depress a person so."

Samuel shifted uncomfortably in the lumpy armchair.

He had just got in from work; it had been a hard day and all he wanted to do was sit, read the newspaper, and wait for his dinner.

"Did you hear me, Sam?"

"Yes, Win, I did hear you, but I'm not sure what I can do about the weather."

"And the rain, Sam. It just never stops raining, day after day."

"I know, darling. But it'll be summer soon. You'll feel better with a bit of sunshine on your body."

He sounded more cheerful than he felt. He knew how unpredictable English summers could be. Chances are there might be the odd sunny day, but the last few summers had been quite dreary, day after chilly day of wind and rain.

“I just wish we were back home. I never felt this lonely and miserable in Harlem.”

Samuel’s heart went out to her and the guilt began to sink in once again.

He loved this woman so much and knew it was his fault that she was so miserable.

It had been his idea to move to England; she had never really wanted to.

At first, it had seemed like an amazing opportunity for a great adventure.

He and their little son, Jeremy, had been so excited to be on the ship. They spent hours walking round the decks, looking out at the ocean. Instead of being able to join them, poor Winifred had gotten very sea sick and she spent most of the four-day crossing stuck in their cabin.

Once they docked in London, life became very uncertain for the little family, and Winifred’s nightmare was confirmed.

From all the stories Samuel had told his wife and son about his time as a G.I. in England during the war, she had expected bunting,welcoming fanfares and streets all but paved with gold.

The reality couldn’t have been more different.

They knew nobody at all in London.

For the first few weeks, they stayed in a cheap hotel near King’s Cross Station.

It had been exciting at first to just hop on a bus and see all the sights: the River Thames, Buckingham Palace, the Houses of Parliament, Trafalgar Square, Piccadilly.

Little Jeremy particularly liked the Tower of London; as a five-year-old boy, he was fascinated by the tales of beheading and of people being hanged, drawn and quartered if they were disloyal to the King or Queen. He didn't really understand what these things meant, he just liked the sound of the stories.

It was only when they really began house hunting that Samuel realised things were different than they had been during the war, when he was a young, attractive G.I. handing out silk stockings and playing his saxophone to impress the girls.

They were now looking for somewhere to rent, and the pickings were slim for people who looked like him and his family.

Their living arrangements didn't have to be posh, or in a particularly smart neighbourhood. After all, they were from Harlem and weren't expecting a palace.

However, they were horrified by what they found through their search.

They bought newspapers and circled all the possible places in the pages, but every time Samuel rang to enquire about viewing a flat, everything was apparently "already let."

"Maybe they just don't understand me because I sound American."

After the first dozen rejections, the couple decided to roam the streets looking for TO LET signs.

They widened their search, getting further away from the centre of town.

"SORRY, NO COLOUREDS."

They were shocked to see these handwritten signs on the windows of so many houses.

There were others that read "NO COLOUREDS OR IRISH," and even a few that went further to say "NO COLOUREDS, NO IRISH, NO CHILDREN."

Samuel was heartbroken. It had been good enough for him and all of his mates to come here and fight for England's freedom during wartime, but their sacrifice now counted for nothing.

He couldn't even get a decent job. He had tried every nightclub in the city, several restaurants, and a couple of offices, but the answer was always the same.

In the end, out of desperation and a need to house and feed his family, he had reluctantly taken a job as a cleaner for London Transport. It was a poorly paid position, but at least it was a start.

"Look mate, you're wasting your time trying to get a place in town. You need to try somewhere like Brixton, there's plenty of your type down there."

John, one of his colleagues at the cleaning depot, spoke kindly.

He knew how hard it was for all these new immigrants. He reckoned that some people were just ignorant, treating other human beings so badly. Most of these new blokes were good workers; they shouldn't be punished just 'cause their skin was a different colour.

"Old Westie knows a lot of people in Brixton. Ask him if he can help you."

Old Westie was the cleaning superintendent. He was about 45 years old and a fine figure of a man, his skin the colour of shiny, black diamonds. He had come to England from the Caribbean some years ago.

"Oh yeah, man. Brixton is the place for you, it'll feel a bit more like home."

It was the first time since his arrival that Samuel hadn't felt like an alien.

"Why don't you come down on Sunday. Bring your family. I'll get my missus to cook something. And I'll make some enquiries about places."

He was as good as his word.

The three of them got the bus from the hotel in King's Cross to Brixton.

It would have been quicker to go by the underground train known as the Tube, but they wanted to see the sights. It was the first time they had ventured south of the river.

The little family all relaxed as they walked from the bus stop to Old Westie's house.

Everywhere they looked, there were people with dark skin, people who looked like them.

"Okay now, before we eat, I've got three places to show you. Nice and handy for the Tube to get to work."

It felt a bit like being back in Harlem — rows of solid brick houses that were divided into rooms, and no signs saying "NO COLOUREDS."

Samuel, Winifred, and Jeremy moved into their new home, the upper half of an old Victorian, red, brick house.

It only had two small bedrooms, a bathroom, a small sitting room, and a tiny kitchen. But it was clean and dry.

Their new landlord, Thomas, was from Jamaica.

He lived downstairs with his family: a wife, four children, and his elderly parents.

"You think you have it hard man. When we came here back in 1948, we were a bit of a novelty. At first they treated us well, even threw a few welcome parties. But as more and more of us arrived, they started to panic. That's when it turned a bit sour."

Samuel and Winifred became fond of Thomas and his family. They were so grateful for their help and friendship.

Before moving to Brixton, they had both felt themselves drowning, drowning in a sea of despair.

Now they were being welcomed with such open arms that they soon felt their desperation receding.

Thomas worked as a bus conductor and his wife, Amy, cleaned offices.

In Jamaica, he had been a college lecturer and she had worked in a bank, but those occupations were closed to them in England.

"I managed to bring a bit of money with me, so as soon as we got jobs, I found this place to buy. It was very run down, derelict really, and dirt cheap. Not many white folk want to buy houses here."

After a few months, the Davis family had settled. Winifred was finally happy. Samuel was doing okay at work, although he hated the job itself. Little Jeremy was thriving. He was enrolled at the local primary school and loved it. He walked to school every day with his new friends.

Amy and her daughters showed Winifred where to shop. They took her to the street markets and introduced her to lots of other women, so she quickly made some friends.

"Sam, now that our Jeremy's doing so well at school, I was thinking of getting a little job.

It doesn't take long to clean this place, and I don't want to just hang around gossiping all day. Amy says there is some work available at her place. What do you think?"

Samuel was thrilled. It was almost like he'd gotten his young bride back. She smiled a lot these days, and seemed genuinely happy in her new home. He came home from work quite late at night, often after 10, but Winifred was always awake with a delicious hot dinner on the table for him and his slippers warming by the fire.

"Of course I don't mind you working my darling; the extra money will really help. But will you still have time to cook my dinner every night?"

So, it was agreed. As long as she promised to keep his stomach full, she could do what she liked.

The office cleaning work was hard, of course. It was nothing like the glamourous job she'd had at the Apollo Theatre in Harlem, where her main tasks had been to look beautiful and to ensure that the performers were happy with their dressing rooms and stage sets.

But Winifred thrived in this new spot in her life. It felt so good to be earning her own money again.

She was on a team with six other women, including Amy. They were all immigrants, all from different parts of the globe, all with the same ambitions. They all wanted to make the very best of the situation they now found themselves in and help provide for their families. They wanted to ensure their kids had bountiful opportunities and chances to succeed in life.

And they all *hated* the English weather.

"Hey, Sam."

He grunted in response. He was reading the sports page of the newspaper. All the men at the depot were obsessed with football, so he tried to keep up with the latest results in order to contribute to their conversations.

"Sam, will you put that damn paper down and pay me some attention?"

He reluctantly laid it aside and looked up at his wife. He still couldn't quite believe that he was married to the most gorgeous, sexiest woman in Brixton. She really was something, especially now that she was happy again. He had been really worried about her when they first came to London; she had seemed to lose all her sparkle and passion for life.

"Samuel, will you stop looking at me like that? You're making me blush. Good thing our Jeremy's all tucked up in bed and can't see the way his daddy is making eyes at me."

Actually, little Jeremy was wide awake, sitting up in his bed in the room next door and listening in on their conversation.

He loved his parents more than anything in the world.

It made him feel so secure and happy to hear them laughing and chattering in the kitchen. Sometimes it would go quiet for a minute or two, and he knew they were kissing.

When he was grown up, he wanted to find a wife just like his mum.

She was beautiful and kind, and almost never shouted at him or his dad.

"Now Sam, just stop your messing about for a minute and listen to me."

He reluctantly released her from his arms.

"You know how you say I'm always moaning about the weather?"

He nodded.

"Well, I'm not the only one. All the girls at work feel the same. I know it's because we all come from hot places, but it sure makes us fed up sometimes. Every day we get soaked going to work, then we come home drenched through and have to dry our wet clothes in front of the fire."

Samuel wondered where this was going.

"Well, we thought maybe we could hire a charabanc and go on a little day trip. All of us, our husbands and kids too. What do you think?"

He was stunned. Instead of just moaning about something he couldn't change for her, she had come up with a solution — and a good one at that.

"Win, I think that's a wonderful idea. I'll ask the boys at the depot tomorrow. Some of them might like to come too! We can hire the bus tomorrow evening."

Jeremy's childhood was punctuated with joyful times like that.

Their day trip turned out to be a coach trip to Brighton, and it was such a success that they repeated it every year.

Sam left his job at the depot and now worked as a bus conductor, getting free travel for his family on London Transport. On weekends and during the school holidays, they could now take a packed lunch and go on little adventures together. Jeremy loved the science museum as he got a little older, though the Tower of London was still his great favourite. Sometimes they went to the zoo in Regents Park, and once they went to Hampton Court Palace, where he teased them by pretending to be lost in the maze.

He was still good friends with all the neighbourhood boys, and they spent hours playing together outside. There were so few cars in the street that they could string a rope from one lamppost to another. The girls would use it for skipping, but to Jeremy and his mates it was a goal post used for football. They were very happy times for him and his family.

As a young boy, Jeremy had no idea that he was considered poor, or that people might treat him differently because of the colour of his skin. All his mates in Brixton were Black. Some had lighter skin, but they were all darker than the average English boy. He remembered Harlem of course, but all his friends had been Black there, too.

He was a very bright kid and had sailed through the eleven-plus exam.

This meant he could go to the grammar school. While he wanted to stay with his friends and to attend the local comprehensive instead, his parents insisted.

"Do you really want to throw away this chance, boy?"

"But Dad, I just want to be with my friends. I won't know anyone at the grammar. I promise to work really hard; I won't mess about and let you down."

His mum was weakening. She just wanted her boy to be happy.

"Look here, son. We just want the best for you. If you can get a good education, it will help you in life — help you to get a decent job, earn good money. I don't want you just ending up on the buses like me."

Samuel had learnt to like his job. Now that he was a bus conductor, he could at least use his charm. He had become very popular, and all the female passengers enjoyed his big, welcoming smile and cheeky manner. He had started playing his saxophone again too; there were often little parties in the neighbourhood and sometimes he even took it to work with him to entertain his workmates during their breaks.

"Dad, I won't end up on the buses. You know I want to be an architect."

Jeremy had been fascinated by architecture since he was quite young.

When they first arrived in London and Jeremy had been so excited by all the big, shiny buildings, they had just attributed the interest to the novelty of a new environment.

However, as he grew, so did his interest in construction and design.

He loved walking along the streets, or better still, viewing the buildings from the top deck of a bus. He would get back from these outings and spend hours drawing child-like impressions of the magnificent structures he had seen.

Of course, his parents won the argument as parents usually do. A few months later, dressed in his smart new blazer, striped cap on his head, and leather satchel under his arm, Jeremy set off for his first day at the grammar school.

He was eleven years old and had never experienced such outward and deliberate racial prejudice before.

"What's that awful smell?"

"Must be coming from the back row, you know, where the new boys are."

At first, Jeremy didn't realise the other kids were talking about him.

He was in a line of about 20 other boys, all looking small and scared in their shiny new uniforms.

"It's that darkie. Don't suppose they wash where he comes from."

Several of the bigger boys tittered.

"Shouldn't allow boys like that to come here, you never know what germs they have."

Their baiting was relentless. Every time they passed him in the corridor, they either pushed him, or stood to one side, holding their noses.

"Mum, I can't go back there. They're just so horrible to me. I don't know why they're picking on me, I've never done anything to them."

Jeremy was shaking.

"Oh love."

There was nothing she could say that would make things any better for her perfect boy.

If only he could have gone to the local school with all his mates. She hated seeing her baby so desperately unhappy.

After he had gone to bed that night, she tackled her husband.

"Sam, the boy is hurting. Please, can we just take him away from that place?"

She gave him an imploring glance, which almost broke him.

"Win, you know the last thing in the world I want is for our boy to be unhappy. But as a young Black boy, this world is not going to be kind to him. Better that he learns that now and develops a thicker skin, because we can't protect him forever."

Samuel wanted to go straight to the school, haul out the culprits, and beat them to a pulp for insulting his son, but he knew from years of bitter experience that it would do no good.

Instead, he had to teach his boy to grow up safe, to become a proud Black man who had intelligence and education to help him offset all the insults and hate he would endure.

Therefore, Jeremy stayed at the grammar school.

The only other Black boy there was in the Sixth Form, a giant from Nigeria.

He took Jeremy aside on the second day and gave him some assurance.

"Now look here, my man. I've been at this place for four years now and I've survived. At first, they were just as bad to me. Beatings and insults every day. But gradually, they gave up. I reckon they're just frightened of us because we're more handsome and better at most sports. Oh, and the girls like us. Just find your passion, and hold onto it.

I'll try to keep an eye out and protect you when I can."

For the first year, Jeremy came home most days with bruises, black eyes, and torn clothes. His books and school cap were stolen on a regular basis, and some days he looked so small and frightened as he left the house that Winifred wanted to run after him, fetch him home, and feed him his favourite fried chicken.

It broke Samuel's heart too, to see his boy suffering so. But he knew from his experiences on the buses, trying to get a house in London, and through his family history, that what Jeremy was facing now was a problem he would have to deal with all his life.

The teachers at the grammar school were mostly kind. There were one or two who obviously resented his presence, but once they realised that he was a hard worker with an excellent brain and a burning desire to learn, they were more supportive.

By the time he was 16 years old, Jeremy was much taller than both his parents.

He was incredibly handsome, very well-mannered, and beautifully spoken.

And still passionate about architecture.

LONDON
1967

They were sitting in the kitchen of the Mews Cottage, drinking cups of lukewarm tea and nibbling on ham sandwiches that no one wanted.

"Well, at least we did him proud. He was always fearful of a Pauper's Grave, even though he had plenty of money at the end."

Sybil spoke quietly, so quietly that they all had to lean towards her to listen.

"I always thought he'd go on forever. Never expected him to go before me."

Daisy squeezed her wrinkled, old hand.

"Oh Sybil, we wouldn't have wanted him to suffer anymore. He was ready to go."

Fred had celebrated his 105th birthday two weeks before he died.

His heart had finally given out after years of struggling. He had never really gotten over losing the love of his life, Frederick

Palmer, the man who rescued him from a life of servitude and had instead given him a life of enduring, celibate love.

"Maybe I should go now too. I've lived too long, seen so many things."

Sybil was 103 herself, still mentally alert but with old legs that didn't work so well anymore.

She and Fred had been living with Daisy in the Mews Cottage for the last ten years.

Daisy was in her 80th year now, but still acted as if she were in her fifties.

Her beloved Blackie had died six years earlier, slowly and horribly from lung cancer that was probably caused by all the years of inhaling coal dust. She missed him terribly.

She had loved him, and only him, since she was just 18.

Blackie had been the one who taught her to read and write. She had been so lost without him in the six years since his passing, and now she had lost Fred, too.

Fred and Sybil had been like parents to her. She had relied on their love and support all her life.

"Oh Sybil, whatever are we going to do without him?"

The two old ladies sobbed in each other's arms while the others looked on helplessly.

Flo and Melissa sat together on the sofa. They were now both in their sixties but still very elegant, even though their black outfits were drab and unflattering.

Fred had died so suddenly that Flo had not had the heart to run up any new mourning clothes for them.

Over the years, Melissa and Flo had become the greatest of friends, much more like loving sisters.

Flo still ran her dress shop on Artillery Passage and Melissa still sent all her Bloomsbury friends to shop there. Flo's designs had become very well-known and sought after, and although her failing eyesight and arthritic hands caused her some difficulty, she still insisted on sewing everything by hand.

Joe, Flo's husband, sat next to them in the old leather armchair.

It was the only one he could get out of easily, so he always preferred to sit there.

He was still a big and handsome man, but since his accident at the docks some ten years earlier, he sometimes had trouble walking and had to rely on a stick.

Today was a bad day.

He was going to miss the old man so much, and he still missed Blackie, too.

They had both been such a support when Flo had been depressed after their Benjamin died, and again with all the trouble over their Vi and that bastard husband of hers.

What a long time ago that all seemed now.

Suddenly, he felt a gentle touch on his shoulder.

It was Matty, the only other man left in their little family, apart from Joe's son, John.

Matty and Ruth still looked younger than their years.

They were both in their eighties now, still living happily with Melissa at Bedford Court Mansions. They led a fairly quiet life these days, no more galavanting every night to the jazz club. But of course, they still drank cocktails, played chess, and entertained their friends. Life had been very good to them all since they left Alabama.

Vi stood in the kitchen. She looked around the room at her family, the family that had loved and supported her through all her traumas.

She had been divorced for many years now.

Blackie had been the one to insist she went to court and make it official.

"If you don't love, he can always try to claim your home, or your money, or even the girls."

She had heard from her dad's family in Southwark that after leaving her, Bert had remarried twice and fathered six more children.

When Old Frederick died, he had left a bequest to her and her brother John. He had said he wanted "to secure you both a better future."

John had used his money to go to university and train as an engineer.

Vi had spent some of hers on a course called, "Department Store Window Dressing," and once the girls started school, she had gone back to her old employers and persuaded them to take her on as a trainee. She had now been there for 15 years and was the senior window dresser.

The lives of Vi's daughters had turned out very different from what she had imagined.

Of course, they had totally different personalities, so maybe it wasn't so surprising.

The years after Bert first abandoned them were so busy that she didn't have time to feel too emotional about the whole thing. Anyway, she had done enough crying before he left to last her a lifetime.

She stayed on at the house on Artillery Passage and realised that if she had indeed moved to Southwark with Bert and tried to raise her children without all the help from her mum, dad, and the others, she probably wouldn't have coped. They had all been truly wonderful — babysitting whenever she needed it, entertaining the girls when she was too tired or fed up to care, and taking them all on day trips or little holidays to the seaside house in Brighton.

She remembered all the times she had taken her girls to Melissa's flat in Bloomsbury.

It had always been Polly who asked all the questions; her sister would just sit quietly, listening.

"Mum, why is Aunty Melissa so nice to us, when she isn't even our real Aunty?"

"Mum, why are Uncle Matty and Aunty Ruth black? I wish I was that colour too, then I could have nice curly hair like them."

"Aunty Ruth, why is Aunty Melissa so kind to everyone? I want to be just like her when I'm grown up. Beautiful, ladylike, generous, and kind. Oh, and maybe rich, too."

On that particular occasion, Polly was about twelve years old (she had been christened Elizabeth Polly, but preferred to be called by her middle name), and Ruth laid down her sewing and looked at the little girl.

"Melissa is a real lady, Polly, in every sense of the word. I have known her since she was a baby and I can tell you that even as a small girl, she was kind to everyone. Didn't matter if they were rich or poor. She acted the same to everyone who came to the house. She never even seemed to notice that us servant girls wore ragged clothes, or that our skins were black; she just loved us."

Matty stopped playing chess and smiled across at his wife.

"Ruth is right, Polly. Melissa is one of the best human beings you will ever meet. She is a truly fine woman, and you will do well in life if you follow her example."

Both of them would have gladly given their lives for Melissa. They were just sad that she had never managed to find another great love after losing her beloved Theo.

Penelope, Polly's sister, was very quiet. She was less curious, more accepting of everything. Never particularly sad and never particularly happy. In fact, she was so quiet, you could forget she was even in the room.

She wasn't at Fred's funeral.

When Blackie died, he had left the two girls a small bequest.

He also left a note, written in his spidery old hand. Once upon a time, he had the most beautiful copperplate handwriting, but as the cancer took hold, his hands got shaky.

"Use this bit of money well, my loves. Enjoy it. Follow your heart and your passion. Always remember how much your old great-grandad loves you."

Polly still had her share, tucked away in her post office account. She was waiting 'til the day she found her passion.

On the other hand and much to everyone's surprise, the day Penny turned 19, she announced that she was using her money to go off and see the world.

"I'm never going to find my passion here in Spitalfields. I think I might go to India."

Within a couple of weeks, she was gone. Her family got the occasional postcard from her, but she never mentioned when (or if) she planned to return.

Now that just about everyone was gone, the house on Artillery Passage seemed very quiet.

John was still in Nottingham. He had done extremely well at university and was now working as an engineer, fulfilling a dream he had had since he was a little boy — a dream that he had only been able to fulfill because of Old Frederick's generosity.

Flo thought about the old man. What a character he had been!

He was the one who had helped her get started with her sewing, all those years ago.

She smiled as she remembered how enthusiastic he had been about helping her choose fabrics and ribbons, and how he had encouraged her to open up her shop. Without him, she would never in a million years have been able to do any of it.

He had used his money so wisely and had helped so many people, and he had loved young Fred so deeply.

It seemed funny now to think of him as "Young Fred," when they had just buried his 105-year-old body.

Flo missed her boy, John, of course, but was glad to know he was doing well with the life he created.

He always came home for the Christmas holidays, but other than that they rarely saw him. Unable to make Fred's funeral, he had sent flowers that now sat on the table in front of where Flo was standing.

As she looked toward the bouquet, she thought more about her dear son. He had always been a rather quiet boy, and now was a useless correspondent, so she had very little idea of how he spent his spare time or who his friends were.

Vi had always been convinced that he preferred men.

"Oh Mum, he'll never get married. I don't know why you're wasting your time hoping for more grandchildren."

This thought hit Flo suddenly.

"Joe?"

Her long-suffering husband looked up from his newspaper. Over the years he thought he had gotten to know everything about this glorious woman he was married to, but she still had the capacity to surprise him every once in a while.

"Yes love?"

"Do you think our John might be, you know, different?"

"What do you mean, different?"

He was stalling for time, not sure how to respond. He had always known that their boy wasn't the marrying kind.

"Oh Joe, don't make me say it."

"I don't think he will ever marry a woman, if that's what you're asking me."

"So is he like the two Freds?"

"Flo, would it really be so bad if he was? They were both good, kind, generous men who wouldn't hurt a fly. Would you rather he was some big ruffian, who fathered six kids by different women and beat them all up when he got home drunk?"

He knew lots of men who behaved exactly like that. Big, strong, working men who treated their wives and families appallingly.

"Oh Joe."

He held her tightly while she sobbed. This glorious, magnificent woman of his. He hated seeing her cry.

"I just can't bear to think he'll never know a love like ours."

From the moment he had married her that snowy Christmas Eve so long ago, she had been the centre of his world. And he knew that she felt the same about him.

"And I wish our Vi could find someone nice, too."

Their daughter had not loved anyone since Bert abandoned her and her babies.

There had been one man she worked with once, one of the store buyers called Peregrine.

He had given her a lift home one evening and she had invited him in for a drink and to meet her parents. Joe had taken an instant dislike to him.

"Did you see the way his eyes were roaming the room, Flo? Checking everything out?"

They had inherited a lot of antique furniture from Old Frederick.

When he had turned his mansion in Marylebone into a home for retired gentlemen, there had been some things he wanted removed.

"Some of these old codgers are a bit unsteady on their feet and will forget to use mats on the polished furniture. I'd much rather the family got it now; no point in waiting 'til I'm dead and it's all ruined."

The Mews Cottage was already pretty full, but Daisy and Blackie had managed to squeeze in a few extra chairs and cabinets. Frederick also arranged to have his piano delivered over there. Daisy was the only one who ever played it, anyway.

Flo and Joe had been delighted to get the rest at Artillery Passage. Their house was big and some of the rooms had never been furnished properly.

Anyway, Peregrine never reappeared in their lives after that night. Vi found out, through another window dresser who worked at the Swan and Edgar department store, that he already had a wife and three children, as well as a mistress installed in a little flat in Soho.

"Joe, I'm a bit worried about Mum and Sybil being on their own in the Mews. They aren't getting any younger and without Fred there, they might be lonely."

"Flo, I suggest you keep those thoughts to yourself. You know your mum doesn't think she's getting old. I know she's gone a bit downhill since your dad died, but let's just leave it for now. We can check on them every day and when the time is right, we can bring them here to live with us."

It took a whole year for Daisy to admit that she couldn't cope.

Sybil was 104 now, and although her mental faculties were still excellent, her hearing was poor and she struggled to get around. They had both moved into bedrooms on the ground floor of the Mews Cottage, as neither of them could manage the stairs easily anymore. All their meals were delivered from Frederick's old place next door; the cooks had all been trained by Sybil, so there was never any doubt about the quality. It had been written into the old man's will that Daisy, Blackie, Sybil, and Young Fred would always have a home in the mansion if they wanted it, and there was a very large sum put aside to cover all their expenses until the day they died.

One day, Flo finally asked Daisy about her and Sybil moving in with them at Artillery Passage.

"I don't want to leave this house. I can't. I feel like I'm letting Blackie down."

Daisy was still grieving for her beloved husband.

It had been seven long years now since he died.

She still missed the sound of his voice.

"Oh Mum. Dad will be with you wherever you are, and you know how he loved it here in Spitalfields. He told me it always felt more like home to him than Marylebone ever did."

She realised she had said the wrong thing, but Daisy just laughed.

"Oh love, I know your dad always felt a bit uncomfortable coming back to the Mews every night with his old horse and cart. He was worried he lowered the tone of the posh neighbourhood. But in fact, everyone here loved him. Do you remember how many people turned out for his funeral? And sent such beautiful flowers?"

Blackie's funeral had been splendid. The hearse had been a glass carriage drawn by two feather-plumed black horses. The undertakers had all worn long frock coats and top hats, and had walked slowly in front of the carriage. People lined the streets, even in Marylebone and Bloomsbury, and men tipped their hats as the funeral cortege passed. Blackie had been both loved and respected throughout his life as a coalman and as a friend.

SOUTH LONDON
1968

Jeremy had a one-track mind.

He had wanted to be an architect since he was a little boy.

In the end, his teachers at the grammar school had been very encouraging and supportive of his desires.

He had worked incredibly hard to win their trust. There were still only a handful of boys like him at the school — working class boys who happened to have black skin.

He had been Deputy Head Boy in his 5th and 6th year, and the mantlepiece at home was covered with all his sporting trophies.

His parents were bursting with pride when they went to his final school prizegiving.

Their boy had done so well, especially considering his inauspicious start so many years ago.

He had been bullied and ridiculed day after day, for months on end, just because of his colour.

But that was all a distant memory now.

"Don't let your past determine your future," his dad had said to him one day when the bullying was at its worst.

"You're a stinking, dirty nigger who should have stayed in America. Your kind knows their place there. We don't want boys like you at our school."

The boy who had said these things was a short, spotty individual called Malcolm.

His dad was a bank manager and they lived in a big house on Wandsworth Common.

He was the ringleader of the mean boys at the grammar school, and the very worst of the bullies.

That was the day Samuel had come home from work to find both his wife and son in tears.

"Oh Sam, I wish we'd never left Harlem."

Winifred had obviously been crying for a long time. Her eyes were all red and puffy.

It absolutely broke his heart.

They had all been so settled and happy until he insisted on sending Jeremy to that school. Perhaps they should have just let him go the local comprehensive with his mates, at least he wouldn't have been picked on there just because he was Black.

Samuel was still working as a bus conductor and had grown to love the job.

It was sociable, he had all his regulars to chat with, and although the hours could be long, he wore a free uniform and got free travel for his family.

London Transport had some great sports and social clubs, and they even held Christmas parties for all the children.

Jeremy had always loved those, especially the jelly and ice-cream and the present they got before they went home.

Winifred was still cleaning offices, but was now running her own team.

In her spare time, she sang in the church choir. The whole family attended church every Sunday, just as they had in Harlem. Jeremy enjoyed Sunday school, and once he was old enough, he joined the church youth club. This gave him the chance to spend time with his old mates. Sometimes, Samuel even played his saxophone in church. The gospel music reminded them of home.

He had seen other boys being bullied on his bus, and it made his blood boil.

It wasn't just Black boys who got picked on, either.

If your tormentors decided you were poor, short, tall, thin, fat, spotty, or smelly, you were a target. Samuel had to break up many fights on the bus. The boys were the ones who fought; the girls usually just used their tongues as weapons.

When he saw his wife and son crying that day, he brought his face down to Jeremy's.

"Look, my lad. I know this is hard for you now. But I promise it won't last forever. One day, these bullies will get bored and leave you alone. Just try and keep working hard at school, do your best, hold your head up high. You may not come from a posh home like some of them, but you are just as good as them." Samuel winked, "and a lot better looking, 'cos you take after your old man."

That made all three of them laugh.

"Don't let your past determine your future."

Those words had stuck in Jeremy's head and he tried his best to follow them. His dad was right, it did get easier.

Now he was 19 years old, had just finished three years at technical college, and was trained to be an architectural assistant. He had thoroughly enjoyed his education and had learnt so much about the field of his dreams.

He knew how hard his parents had worked so he could study. He just wanted to make them proud. but knew he still had years and years to go before becoming a proper architect.

One of his lecturers at the tech had managed to get him a placement at the LCC (London County Council) Architects' Department.

If he impressed them and continued to work hard after another four or five years of training on the job, he might qualify.

He often went on site visits with his colleagues.

They were all remarkably expert, committed architects, sure of their own abilities.

In fact, it was often said that the most gifted and talented architects of the period had worked at the LCC at some point in their career.

Locally, it was a time of great change, a challenge to rebuild parts of the city where bombsites and slum clearances had to be replaced with new dwellings.

Dwellings for ordinary people — not just for the rich.

He learnt about floor-to-ceiling windows and skylights and how to design more open-plan homes without so many pokey little rooms.

One of his mentors told him that "people do not desperately desire to be housed on large estates or in towering blocks, no matter how imaginative the design or convenient the dwelling." He learned so much from these older men and fell in love with his work even more, passionate about creating imaginative spaces for people to make their homes.

It was truly incredible how determined he was to fulfill his dream, and continue the journey he had embarked on when he first came to London at five years old.

EAST LONDON
1968

Daisy sat on the edge of the bed, holding the hand of the old lady who was dying.

She watched as Sybil's chest went up and down, up and down, with each laboured breath.

Tears poured down her wrinkled old face.

Sybil was 104 now, so dying was inevitable.

Daisy was hardly a spring chicken herself at 81, but she couldn't bear the thought of losing her oldest and dearest friend. Sybil was the one who had been with her through thick and thin, quite truthfully, since the day she was born.

The older woman was Daisy's last link to Polly, a mother she could barely remember who had died when she was just three years old.

"Oh Flo, what am I going to do without her? I just can't bear the thought of it. It's only been a year since Fred died. I can't believe I'm about to lose them both."

Daisy's daughter was sitting on the other side of the bed. She loved the old lady too; Sybil had been like a grandmother to her.

The two older women had been living with Flo and Joe at Artillery Passage for just a few months.

Daisy had been desperate to stay at the Mews Cottage, but after struggling for almost a year she had admitted defeat. That's when they moved in with Flo and her family.

It had been a very happy few weeks until Sybil got sick. She had gone downhill very quickly, but refused to go to hospital, insisting she wanted to die in her own bed.

"Mum, just try and think of all the happy times. Let's talk about them, so Sybil can hear us. The doctor said that people's hearing is often the last thing to go."

Daisy wasn't sure if this was true, but she did as her daughter suggested and the next couple of hours were spent reminiscing about old times.

She was certain she saw Sybil smile once or twice. Then, she was gone.

Just one month later, Daisy succumbed to a nasty bout of influenza, and they lost her too.

Flo was too upset to speak at her mum's funeral.

She sat in the front row of the little chapel, holding Joe's hand tightly and dabbing her eyes constantly with one of her mum's old cotton handkerchiefs. It still smelt of the lavender spray Daisy had been so fond of.

Vi tried to say a few words, but she too welled up with tears and was unable to continue.

Matty walked to the front and stood beside her. He gave her hand a gentle squeeze before he spoke. The tall, still good-looking Black man and the small, beautiful, young divorcee.

"All of us here loved Daisy. She was a very special lady. And I know we all have our own memories of her. To me, she was the epitome of goodness. Despite her rough start in life, she always looked on the bright side. She gave everybody the benefit of the doubt, always assuming there was good in us all. When I first came to this country and met Daisy, I thought she was one of the finest, kindest women I had ever seen. If she hadn't already been married to Blackie, I would have swept her off her feet and married her myself."

A ripple of laughter ran through the room. A few people turned around to look at his wife, Ruth, to see her reaction to his words. They could see her smiling through her tears.

"I have had the honour and the pleasure of calling Daisy Bacon my friend for almost 50 years; I just wish we didn't have to say goodbye to her today."

He escorted a weeping Vi back to her seat.

"May I say a few words?"

Polly walked to the front and laid her hand gently on the oak coffin, taking care not to squash the beautiful flowers.

"My great-grandma, Daisy, was the most wonderful person in the world. We all loved her so much and will miss her terribly. Somehow she never seemed like an old person, so I think we're all shocked that she's gone. She never had the luxury of a mother or a father when she was growing up, but she made sure that we all had the most wonderful family life.

Her and my great-grandad, Blackie, were everything that people should be. I'm just so grateful that I knew her and I really hope I can make her proud. As proud as we all were of her."

It took a few weeks before any semblance of order was restored to Artillery Passage.

Although Daisy and Sybil had only been living there for a few weeks, the house seemed empty without them.

Flo worked downstairs in her shop every day. Sewing had always been her solace in times of trouble.

Joe kept a careful eye on his wife. He knew how much her mum had meant to her.

John had come home for the funeral and stayed on a few extra days to help cheer up his mum. Now he had gone too, back to Nottingham and the life of which his family knew so little.

Vi had gone back to work as well. Planning her shop window displays was a good way of taking her mind off of sad thoughts.

Polly was now working as a shorthand typist at a big office in the West End.

She had inherited the sewing gene that seemed to be passed down to every alternate generation in the family. Flo had rather hoped she could persuade her granddaughter to take over the shop, so that she could put her feet up a bit.

"After all love, your name is already on the window."

When Flo had first opened the dress shop, she had surprised them all by calling it "Polly's." She had named it after her grandmother after all, who had died before she was ever born.

She had been running the shop for over 40 years now and wanted to ease up a bit and have more time to spend with Joe. She was aware that he had always taken a back seat to her business, although he would never dream of complaining.

"Your granddad and I would quite like to spend a bit more time together down in Brighton."

Fred and Sybil had bequeathed the Brighton town house to Daisy and after her death, it was passed to her daughter.

Although Polly loved sewing, often helping her grandmother in the shop on Saturdays and during the school holidays, she had no intention of working there once she left school.

She wanted to get out into the big wide world and make her own life.

Going to university was never an option. She was not naturally academic and anyway, almost no one from their neighbourhood went on to higher education. Instead, during her final year at school she decided to take the typing lessons offered as part of the curriculum. She quite enjoyed them and was a fast learner. When the term was over, she enrolled at the local technical college to do a Pitman Shorthand and Typing Course.

After that, she landed a good job in the city.

She had promised her mum and Flo that she would continue to look after the shop on the weekends and during her paid annual leave.

"Grandma, do you think you could make me a new dress?"

Flo wondered how many times she had heard that request.

"Of course my darling girl, when do you need it by? Have I got any material that will do?"

She was used to Polly rummaging around in her piles of fabric; she had done it for years, even when she was quite small and wanted new clothes made for her dolls.

"Oh no, don't worry Grandma, I picked some up in the market during my lunch hour today."

Polly delved into her bag and brought out a length of emerald-green satin.

Flo was dismayed to see the cheap, shiny fabric. She knew it would be a disaster to sew.

"What kind of style did you think of having, love?"

"Oh, just a little sheath dress, quite short, so it shouldn't take you long. I didn't bother to buy a zip or any thread, 'cos I knew you'd probably already have the right colour. Oh and if you could possibly make it by tomorrow night, that would be lovely! I'm going to the Locarno."

The older woman sighed. These youngsters had no idea. They could be so selfish, even the nicest ones like her Polly. They thought money grew on trees and that everything should be available for their convenience. It had been so different in her day.

Of course, so much had happened in the last ten years or so that to these kids, everything probably seemed so easy. Man could now go into Space and fly across oceans instead of spending weeks on ships.

Young women wore mini-skirts and burned their bras. They could even go on the pill to prevent unwanted pregnancies. She knew that Vi was happy about that in particular; she didn't want either of her girls making the same mistake she had by getting in the family way before they were married. And as for their music! Sometimes she and Joe would have to yell up the stairs to get Polly to turn it down.

"Hey Grandma, do you want to listen to my new record? It's really fab, the latest Beatles LP, called Sgt. Pepper's Lonely Hearts Club Band."

Polly had all The Beatles's records, as well as all the records from The Rolling Stones, The Animals, and Four Tops.

Every week that girl seemed to discover something new to spend her money on, and she didn't seem to take much of anything seriously. Despite this attitude, Flo knew she must have been good at her job and obviously worked hard in the office, because she had just gotten a small pay raise. This, of course, meant she had even more money to spend on herself, and plenty of free time to spend it.

As she grew up, Polly didn't have a particular interest in the world around her, either.

When she was younger, she had loved to listen to Granddad Joe as he spoke of the Cuban Missile Crisis, the Vietnam War, the "Ban the Bomb" campaign, and the rise of the Berlin Wall.

These days, she only seemed to care about her music, the length of her skirts, how to do her eye make-up like Twiggy, and what to wear when she went dancing every Friday and Saturday night.

When she wasn't listening to her records, she played BBC Radio One, a new station established by the BBC to attract young listeners and fill the gap that had been left by all the old pirate stations, like Radio Luxembourg.

Melissa, Matty, and Ruth came to the house on Artillery Passage every Wednesday afternoon.

Flo always closed the shop at one o'clock on Wednesdays so they could spend the whole afternoon together. She and Joe so looked forward to those times with their friends.

"I'm a bit worried about our Polly."

"She doesn't seem to have anything much in that pretty little head of hers except for boys, music, and clothes."

Matty nearly choked on his tea.

"Oh Flo, that's just normal. She is a teenager, after all."

"And that's another thing, Matty. Where did this word "teenager" ever come from?"

"In my day you were just a child, then when you went to work you became a young adult.

We never had fancy titles to make us feel special. And we gave all our wages to our mum and dad and they just gave us back a bit of pocket money."

Joe snorted.

Now his wife was on her high horse!

He knew how she felt about Vi not insisting that Polly paid something for her keep.

But Vi's argument back to her was that *they* had never made her pay her way in their home, so why should she get Polly to do it?

Everyone knew that this was Flo's pet subject, and that she could wax lyrical about it for hours if left unchecked.

"Anyway, we have more important things to discuss today."

Melissa was the only one brave enough to stop Flo mid-sentence.

"Can you believe they've actually killed him? And so soon after Martin too."

She was referring to the assassination of Bobby Kennedy, which occurred so soon after the assassination of Martin Luther King, Jr.

"I can't believe it's happened again. Another Kennedy gone."

When President John F. Kennedy had been assassinated in Dallas, Texas, in 1963, the whole world had been shaken. Now his brother Robert was gone too, gunned down by a lone assassin.

Martin Luther King, Jr. had been shot and killed on 4th April 1968, in Memphis, Tennessee.

Bobby Kennedy lost his life on 6th June, the same year.

They had all admired Martin Luther King, Jr. greatly.

Though Melissa, Ruth, and Matty had made their lives in England so long ago, they were still American, and of course still followed the politics of the country. Besides that, everyone drinking tea in Flo's kitchen that Wednesday afternoon abhorred racial prejudice.

Being Black meant that Ruth and Matty had an even greater and immensely personal understanding of how the civil rights movement affected people's lives in America and elsewhere.

"Do you remember his speech, just months before the president was killed?

Slowly, they each recited their favorite parts of the famous, "I Have a Dream" speech.

"I have a dream that one day... the sons of former slaves and the sons of former slave owners will be able to sit down together at the table of brotherhood." "...they will not be judged by the colour of their skin but by the content of their character." "I have a dream that one day, down in Alabama... little Black boys and Black girls will be able to join hands with little White boys and White girls as sisters and brothers."

These were the words that resonated the most with the three Americans, Melissa as the granddaughter of a former slave owner and Matty and Ruth as descendants of former slaves.

"Surely now, after all these years, things will change. The civil rights movement has managed to abolish segregation, so maybe at last things will start to improve! Maybe the death of that good man will make things better."

Flo spoke through her usual sunny and optimistic outlook on life.

She had never experienced racial hatred first-hand, so had no real idea how it could erode a person's whole life, how it could destroy their well-being, trust, and self-respect.

Matty, Ruth, Melissa, and Joe all exchanged knowing smiles. Each loved Flo dearly, but none of them were under any illusion that she truly had the ability to understand. She had been cosseted by them all, and others, all her life. She was the first one in their extended family to have known no real hardship, which of course, made her family proud of their progress. Apart from losing her baby Benjamin, she had led a life that allowed her to be sunny, having never suffered the privation that comes with poverty or illegitimacy, as her mother and grandmother had done so long ago. And she had most certainly never experienced discrimination of colour or creed.

Her husband, Joe, had a little more understanding of the hard parts of life.

As a docker growing up in the slums of the East End, he had known the cruelty of snobbery. Poverty was a different cross to be borne, and he could not begin to imagine having to suffer that as well as racial discrimination.

Taking in their looks, Flo was desperate to change the subject.

She just wanted a happy afternoon with her husband and dearest friends.

"Shall I make some more tea?"

"Why are you so worried about Polly?"

Ruth spoke quietly. She was a gentle woman, now in her eighties. She had often helped Flo with her dressmaking in the past, and during the time they knew each other and worked together, the two women had gained each other's trust and respect.

"Oh Ruth."

Joe had heard it all before, so many times.

"Matty, do you fancy a game of chess? We could go into the dining room and leave the girls to it in here."

Matty was relieved.

He thought Flo fussed too much, but didn't want to risk saying the wrong thing and upsetting her. Better that he was out of the way; Ruth would fill him in on all the details later.

"Oh Ruth, I just worry that she's got no interests, no spark, and I don't really like some of the boys she hangs around with."

"Oh dear. What's wrong with them?"

"Well, there was this nice lad called Peter. She met him years ago at the church youth club. He's from a good home, nice family. I think he's a bank clerk now. But she said he's boring and doesn't like her going dancing or to the coffee bar."

Melissa chuckled.

"Well I don't reckon he would have fitted very well into this family then, Flo. He sounds rather serious. You know how we all like to dance and Matty still plays his saxophone like a young man!

He probably wouldn't approve of our cocktails, either. And I agree with Polly about the coffee bars; they're wonderful places. We always used to go to Moka on Frith Street, but now we often go to the one just round the corner, on Store Street. It's run by a lovely young Italian man. Mind you, Matty always says that Ruth and I only go there to make eyes at all the handsome young waiters."

She and Ruth fell about laughing, and Matty and Joe, who were eavesdropping from the other room, exchanged a grin.

"Oh Flo, don't worry so. She's still so young and should be out having fun and spending all her money on make-up, records, and clothes. Sometimes I wish I had done a bit more living before I met my Theo."

Melissa had never remarried after Theo. He was the love of her life, and after he died she had been bereft, unable to contemplate life without him.

Without the love and support of her beloved Ruth and Matty, she was not sure she would have wanted to survive.

Their "little trip" to England in 1921 had changed all their lives for the better.

But in all her life, she had never found anyone good enough to take Theo's place. He had been gone, and she alone, for almost 50 years.

"But Melissa, lots of her friends are already getting married and having babies. I don't want her to end up as a lonely old spinster, still working in the typing pool. I just want her to be happy."

"Flo, sometimes getting married doesn't make you happy. Look at your Vi, she's much happier on her own."

It was true.

After the initial shock of being abandoned by Bert when Penelope was just a baby and she was pregnant with Polly, Vi had flourished.

Once the girls were old enough to go to school, she had re-trained as a shop window dresser and was eager to go to work every day.

She had never remarried, but still enjoyed a good social life. Her ex-husband Bert enjoyed his social life as well, fathering six more children and getting divorced twice.

"And I don't like some of the boys she hangs around with. Some of them are even mods and drive 'round town on their scooters. They pick her up and roar away, off to do goodness knows what!"

Melissa laughed.

"Well, just be grateful they're not rockers who wear dirty old leather jackets and rev up their bikes outside the house. Your neighbours would make a fuss then, I bet."

They were only teasing Flo. They understood her worries. Some of these modern young men did seem to be a little wild, with their long hair and droopy moustaches. Melissa and Ruth had seen them in the coffee bar, had seen how they looked at all the pretty young girls in their tiny little skirts.

Matty had tried to explain to them that boys had been that way forever.

"They're no different than how we were. Back in the '20s in the club, we used to ogle all the women in just the same way. The only difference is that we were wearing suits and the ladies' dresses were longer. Some of the older guys even used to tell me how back in the old times, they would hang around street corners to catch a glimpse of ladies' ankles when they lifted up their skirts to keep them dry as they walked through puddles."

No matter what her friends told her, Flo was unconvinced.

"I just wish she could meet someone nice, someone who would love her properly and take care of her like my Joe has done for me all these years."

"Do you ever hear from Penelope?"

It had been nearly two years now since Polly's sister had gone away.

"Not often. She's not very good at writing letters. Sometimes we get the odd postcard, but of course you've seen all those. Apparently she's still in India, at some place you go to learn meditation and yoga. I don't know if she'll ever come back. She seems to have made some friends out there and apparently she earns a bit of money making dresses and long scarves."

They all smiled at the irony of this.

Both of Vi's girls had inherited the ability to sew from their great-great-great grandmother. Surely Penny could have stayed put in Spitalfields if she was just going to end up as a dressmaker!

"Does Polly have a regular boyfriend?"

"I don't know, Melissa. There always seems to be different ones coming to pick her up.

But they all look the same to me; there's nothing different or interesting about any of them."

"Did you say she was going to the Locarno? The Streatham Locarno? Oh Ruth, do you remember when Matty took us there all those years ago? I think it was 1944. There were lots of American GIs there and they taught us how to jitterbug. It was such a lovely place to go. Wasn't there a theatre there too, where we used to take the girls to see the pantomimes?"

SOUTH LONDON 1969

The Streatham Locarno was no longer quite the grand venue that Melissa remembered from 1944, but it was still a great place to go, dance, and listen to good music.

It was a wet Friday night in South London.

Polly stepped off the Number 159 bus with her best friend, Janice.

Janice worked with her in the typing pool, and it hadn't taken long for them to click.

Tonight, they had been a bit later than usual in getting the bus.

Usually on a Friday, they would take their best clothes to work, get changed in the office cloakrooms at the end of the day, have a drink at the local pub with their co-workers, then get the bus down to Streatham. But today, because Polly was desperate to wear her new green dress, they had to go back to Artillery Passage first.

"I do hope she's managed to finish it."

"Oh Poll, don't be cross if she hasn't. You didn't give her much notice."

Janice lived in Islington with her three brothers, two sisters, mum, and granddad.

Her father had left them when she was just 10 years old.

They were a close-knit, loving family, but money was always tight. There certainly wasn't enough for her to splash out on a new dress every time they went dancing, like Polly seemed to. But she didn't mind. Polly was a generous friend and always passed on her dresses when she tired of them, so Janice had a wardrobe full of them now.

Tonight, they both felt quite glamorous.

Janice was wearing a pretty pink Lurex halter-neck dress, one of Polly's cast-offs.

The sparkly fabric quite suited her.

She was a very pretty girl with long, naturally blonde, straight hair that parted in the middle. She was slightly shorter than Polly, so the mini-dress stopped about three inches above her knee. When her friend had worn it, it had only just skimmed her thigh.

Flo had originally made it longer, but had been persuaded by her granddaughter to cut another few inches off the bottom.

Polly was wearing her new, shiny, emerald-green dress (which wasn't as flimsy as it might have been, thanks to Flo adding a lining of fine cotton lawn).

Grandma Flo, as always, had been as good as her word and had made the dress in time for the girls' night out.

Polly knew she could have made it herself, and probably should have, as her grandma always had plenty of other sewing to do. But it would never have looked this good.

No wonder the shop had been so successful; her grandma was a whizz with fabric. Just give her any old piece of material and she could run up a fabulous dress in no time.

They were excited as they queued up outside the Locarno Ballroom.

It was a shame it was raining, even though it was really only a drizzle.

Some of the other girls in the queue were wearing those funny little plastic rain bonnets to protect their locks, but Polly and Janice were sheltering under an umbrella.

Finally, it was their turn to enter. They could hear the music blaring and the clink of glasses. The air was stiflingly hot and the dancefloor was already crowded.

The two girls joined the queue for the ladies' cloakroom. The excitement in there was palpable.

Dozens of girls, dressed up to the nines, chattering and giggling as they applied black eyeliner and pale-pink lipstick.

"Here, did you see that Simon? He thinks he's Jack the Lad. Just 'cos he's got a Triumph Herald."

"Well just make sure if he offers you a lift home that you jump out quickly, before he tries to pin you down in the front seat. Marjorie had to fight him off last week."

"Mind you, he is rather handsome."

Janice smiled. She knew exactly who they were talking about.

Just a couple of months ago, Simon had offered her a lift home, and before she knew where she was, he had parked up on a side street and was trying to kiss her.

But now she had her Terence.

She had met him on the dancefloor six weeks ago, and it had been pretty much love at first sight. Well, for her at least. He seemed to be taking a while to talk about love, although he did seem quite fond of her, especially when they had a quick kiss behind the bushes at the end of her road. He was never really satisfied with just a kiss of course, and she usually had to grab hold of his big hands when they started roaming all over her body. She wanted to wait until she was married. She didn't want to have a shotgun wedding like her sister, Brenda. She wanted to walk down the aisle in a beautiful, white dress.

"C'mon Jan, hurry up. I want to get out there before all the best boys are gone."

Janice knew that her Terence would be on the dancefloor already. He was such a good dancer, much better than her. He went to the Locarno at least four times a week.

She just hoped that he didn't dance with any other girls when she wasn't there.

The boys, and even some men as old as thirty, were lined up on one side of the dance floor. They were all propping up the bar and drinking pints of beer.

Eyeing the talent.

The girls were on the other side, giggling in small groups and sipping their drinks.

Some had Babycham, a few sipped on orange juice, and others had vodka and lime or a Rum and Coke.

Janice could see Terence standing in the middle of the dancefloor, gyrating his hips and looking like a young Greek god.

"C'mon Jan, let's dance."

Polly led her over to an empty spot underneath the glittering chandelier. They began to dance, swaying their hips in time to the beat.

And then she spotted him — the man she would marry.

LONDON
CHRISTMAS DAY
1969

Melissa looked around her sitting room, studying the faces of everyone there.

All the best people in her life, what a blessing they all were.

She was in her 69th year now, and she knew that Ruth and Matty had big plans to celebrate her 70th next year. They thought it would be a secret, that she would be surprised, but she had overheard them plotting with Flo.

She glanced toward the newest members of the family that took more than 50 years to create and thought again about how their group had expanded once again, this time by three.

She would never forget that day, the day Polly introduced him to them all.

"Mum, could you please invite Aunty Melissa, and Matty and Ruth, to tea on Sunday?

I want you all to meet someone."

Vi had reluctantly looked up from the book she was reading, *I Know Why The Caged Bird Sings,* by an American writer called Maya Angelou. She had been engrossed with the autobiography and wanted to finish it so she could pass it on to Ruth to read.

"Okay love, of course I will. I'm sure they'll be happy to come, especially if your granddad makes some of his ginger cake."

Joe had developed a passion for cooking. Well, not *cooking* exactly, but he had become rather good at baking and his ginger cake had become something legendary.

"Who are you bringing? Is it Janice and her fiancé? What was his name again?"

Janice had finally gotten Terence to agree to an engagement. He had been a little reluctant, until she had allowed him to slip his hand inside her blouse. Of course, he had wanted more.

"Sorry, love. I just want to be a virgin when I get married. I'm sure you'd prefer a wife that hasn't been with anyone else."

He had eventually produced a little diamond ring and a date had been set for a Saturday in March of the following year. He still tried to persuade her to do more, to "go all the way," but she refused.

"No Mum, it's not Janice. And her fiance's name is Terence, by the way."

Polly wasn't sure about him.

Okay, he was good-looking and a good dancer, but she didn't think he was good enough for her best friend. He was too cocky and not very honest. He had once told Janice that he worked in a bank, implying that although he was just a clerk now, he was in line for a promotion.

They had since found out that he was only a cleaner there. On top of that, he still went to the Locarno four times a week, and Polly wasn't sure that he was very loyal to Janice.

"I want you all to meet my new boyfriend."

"I really, really like him, Mum. I think it's serious this time. And I know he feels the same."

It had been a Sunday in late September.

The trees were turning colour and losing their leaves.

Everyone was assembled at Artillery Passage and sitting in the parlour.

Joe's renowned ginger cake sat on the table, together with the best bone china tea set.

Polly could hear their chatter as she mounted the stairs.

"Hello everybody. I'd like you all to meet my new boyfriend. We're thinking of getting married and want your blessing."

Afterwards, Melissa wished she had had a camera handy to record the surprise on all their faces.

"This is Jeremy."

They had met at the Locarno.

She had noticed him straight away.

He was tall, taller than her, which was a bonus. She was fed up with dating short men.

She had inherited Grandma Flo's statuesque build and was nearly six feet tall.

She must have been staring at him for age, before he came over.

"Hello, would you like to dance?"

His voice was like velvet. He was well spoken, not like some of the ruffians she usually met.

Janice had to poke her; suddenly her whole body seemed frozen.

She smiled weakly, looking up at his handsome black face.

"Yes, she does want to." Janice shoved her into his arms.

They had been seeing each other for a few months before she took him to meet her family, though she had met his already. He collected her from the office one afternoon and they had caught the bus to Brixton. She had been surprised but not concerned, to find herself the only person with a white skin as they walked from the bus stop to his house.

"Hello my dear, welcome to our home."

Winifred was charming and seemingly unsurprised to find her son bringing a tall, White girl to the house.

In fact, he had told both his parents about her already.

At first they were not very happy at the news, especially when he told them how serious he was about the girl.

"Oh son, you're opening a mighty fine can of worms. Have you really thought about this?"

His dad was anxious. Working on the buses, he still saw so much racial tension.

Samuel also remembered the early years when Jeremy had started at the grammar school and had been bullied mercilessly just because he was Black.

"Can't you find a nice girl 'round here, son? There's some lovely looking ones down at the church. More like you."

But once they met Polly, it all changed. She was such a fine girl, good-looking and caring, and they could see why their boy had fallen in love with her.

However, they were worried about meeting her family. She may not mind about the colour of their skins, but what would her East End family think?

Polly had not thought to mention to her family that Jeremy was Black.

She hadn't really talked about him much, other than to briefly allude to her new "boyfriend."

She had grown up knowing and loving Matty and Ruth as part of her family, so to her it had seemed quite natural.

As she said the words, "This is Jeremy," she could feel the atmosphere in the room begin to change.

Maybe it was her imagination, but she thought she heard a deep chuckle coming from the big armchair in the corner. Matty's seat.

Her granddad, Joe, was the first one to recover his senses. Quickly, he leapt out of his chair and shook Jeremy's hand.

"Hello lad. Welcome. Glad to meet you."

One by one, they stood up to greet him.

Polly looked over to the corner where Matty was still sitting.

She could see his shoulders moving as if he was laughing, but when she got closer, she realised he was crying.

Tears were pouring down his old black face.

"Oh Uncle Matty, what's wrong?"

He pulled her close to him, so close that she could feel the wetness of the tears on his face.

"Nothing's wrong, my darling. Quite the opposite. You have made an old man very happy. Never, in my lifetime, did I expect to see a white girl I loved marry a Black man. A Black man like me."

It had been a very happy afternoon. By the end of it, they had all fallen a little bit in love with Jeremy. He was a fine young man who obviously made their girl very happy.

Now it was Christmas Day of 1969, and they were all together in the mansion flat in Marylebone.

It was the first time since the engagement party that they had all seen Samuel and Winifred, Jeremy's parents.

Melissa wasn't sure if she had ever seen Matty and Ruth smile so much.

From the moment Jeremy had come into their lives, it was as if another door had opened for them, a door that none of them with white skin could ever enter.

They had had an enormous lunch. Melissa had announced that, as it was a very special and much larger gathering this year, she was getting the caterers in.

"That way, none of us have to spend hours working away in the kitchen to prepare all the food. We can all just relax and enjoy each other's company."

It had been a marvellous idea.

The day had started with champagne at eleven o'clock. It was now three in the afternoon and they were all lazing around, their stomachs full to bursting after all the delectable food.

She had filled the house with red poinsettias and garlands of green ivy.

The big Christmas tree in the bay window was decorated with hundreds of white baubles. Melissa had done a tree up like this every year since Theo died. It reminded her of the Christmas tree at his father's plantation house in Alabama, the house where her engagement to her beloved Theo was announced so many years ago.

She listened to the little pockets of conversation going on around her.

"Well, I was thinking of Brussels lace, but our Polly says she wants velvet."

That was Flo and Ruth, discussing the fabric for Polly's wedding dress.

"Come on love, please think about it. It makes a lot of sense; you know it does."

She wasn't sure what Vi and Polly were talking about, but it sounded quite serious.

Jeremy's deep voice came next.

"Rocketing budgets, out of control, will kill off this development before it starts. Stupid men chasing their egos while people have to live in substandard housing. And of course, all the trade unions don't help. They will destroy this country, take my word for it."

She could hear the anger in Joe's voice as he replied.

"We break our backs so the rich man in Belgravia can have fresh pineapple on his plate and Indian tea in his china cup."

Joe was spouting his trade union doctrine to poor young Jeremy.

He was a staunch union man, as most dockers were.

"You're too young and privileged to understand this, Jeremy, but to the ordinary working man, the unions and the Labour Party have been our salvation. I don't expect you to agree with me as I know you've never had to get up and go to work at 5:30 on a cold and dark winter morning, with no breakfast to warm you and hardly enough clothes on to stop you freezing to death on the docks. If you had done that, even just once my lad, you would understand."

Of course, Jeremy did understand.

He hadn't meant to upset his future grandfather-in-law, but he was passionate about housing and got very frustrated by all the red tape he had to deal with in his job at the council.

"Sorry sir, I shouldn't have said all that. Of course I respect you and all the other working men who have fought so hard to make this country what it is."

"Nonsense lad. I'm glad to see you have a bit of fire in your belly. Of course we'll never agree on all this, but I like it that you're passionate about what you believe. Let's shake hands on it and have another glass of port. As it's Christmas."

She could see Ruth and Winifred deep in conversation. It made her happy to see that Ruth had found a new friend.

Samuel and Matty were sitting on the old leather sofa. Actually, they were sprawling rather than sitting after all the food and drinks they had consumed. One was at either end, with their feet up on the matching footstool.

"Hey Melissa! Did you know Samuel plays the sax too?"

Both men smiled at her.

"That's wonderful! Perhaps one day you can do a little concert for us."

"Actually, we were thinking we might play something at the wedding."

LONDON
EARLY APRIL 1970

Polly and Jeremy were married on a beautiful, but rather chilly spring day.

The sun shone all morning, but then the sky turned grey. As they were coming out of the church, it started to snow.

Standing on the steps of the old stone church, Jeremy leant down and brushed away a few snowflakes that had landed on his new wife's beautiful face.

She tilted her head and laughed, as he kissed her gently on her cold nose.

Flo stood watching them and felt a sense of déjà vu.

"Oh Joe, that's what you did on our wedding day."

She was very emotional.

Weddings were always wonderful of course, but this one was so special.

You only had to look 'round the church to see that. All the aisles were packed. Family, friends, and workmates.

Black and White, Black and White. All mixed up and happy in each other's company.

As for the bride and groom — what a spectacular pair.

Flo was glad now that Polly had insisted on velvet; it suited her so well.

Jeremy was wearing a navy-blue velvet suit. He had bought it on Carnaby Street at one of the fashionable menswear shops. He was slim, six feet, three inches tall, and very handsome in the blue suit. With his crisp, white shirt and matching blue tie, he looked like a film star.

And Polly. There had never been a more beautiful bride.

"Grandma, I really want a velvet dress. And I want a cape like you had, with fur 'round the hood."

Polly had fished out the photo of Flo and Joe on their wedding day, from Christmas Eve, 1924. How young they had looked.

So, she had done as her granddaughter wanted.

Now, there she was with her handsome new husband, looking absolutely stunning and so happy.

Her bridesmaid, Janice, looked pretty too. She wore a yellow dress with a matching cape.

The cape hid her swollen belly; Flo had designed it well.

Janice and Terence had been married just a month before. He had finally persuaded her, after a drunken Christmas party, to give up on her virginity plan. She seemed happy to be married, but Flo was worried for her. She had seen the way Terence eyed up some of the young girls at Polly and Jeremy's wedding when he thought his wife wasn't looking.

"Doesn't our Polly look magnificent?"

Melissa suddenly appeared beside her. Wearing a pale-blue suit with a fur collar and cuffs, she looked much younger than her 70 years.

"I bet you're glad she had her own way now, aren't you Flo?"

Flo had been so disappointed all those years ago when her daughter Vi had to get married, already pregnant, and refused to wear a white gown.

Polly's dress was probably her last chance. Penelope was still living in India and unlikely ever to return, so this velvet dress would be her final swansong.

She was struggling to sew nowadays. Her eyesight was failing and her arthritis sometimes made it so her hands were in too much pain to do fancy work. Vi had bought her a sewing machine, but she still preferred to sew by hand when her body allowed.

LONDON
1974

Polly and Jeremy had been happily married for four years now.

They lived in the old Mews Cottage in Marylebone, the one that Old Frederick had given to Daisy on her wedding day.

The day she married Blackie, the coalman, back in 1905.

The house had been empty since Daisy died.

Flo had inherited it of course, but she was happy in the house on Artillery Passage.

She had suggested that Vi move into it, but she refused.

"No Mum, it needs a family. I would just rattle around in it and be lonely."

"Anyway, I'm happy living here with you and Dad. Unless you want to get rid of me?"

So, on Christmas Day when they were all at Melissa's, Vi had suggested to Polly that her and Jeremy have the cottage.

"Your grandma and I thought we could give it to you as a wedding present. That's what Old Frederick did for Daisy, so we thought it would be fitting. But we would like it to be just in your name, love. That way you will always have some security, something of your own. Do you think Jeremy would mind?"

He didn't, of course. He was a modern man who thought women were his equals.

They had been living at the Mews since they returned from their honeymoon.

The old house was a little dated but structurally sound, so they had just made a few cosmetic changes. They kept most of the old furniture, although some of it was looking a little worse for wear.

Their precious little daughter was just three years old; she had been born exactly a year after their wedding day.

She was their sunshine, a joy to the entire family. Everyone doted on her.

One day while sitting on the damp grass, Polly and her daughter made daisy chains.

One large white hand and one small black one.

"Mum, why am I called Daisy?"

"Well my love, you come from a long line of strong women. The first Daisy, your great-great-grandmother, the one you're named after, was one of those women."

The little girl beamed. She wanted to be strong too.

"Mum, was that Daisy black like me?"

THE END

REFERENCES

Uncle Tom's Cabin, a novel by Harriet Beecher Stowe.
(Published 1852)

Quotes from Harriet Tubman, escaped slave and civil rights activist.
(1822-1913)

Martin Luther King, Jr., civil rights activist, "I Have A Dream" speech
(1963)

The Report of the Royal Commission on Population
Frank W. Notestein
(1949)

Did you enjoy this book? Please leave a review!

Your feedback is important to me. Once you've finished this book, please head over to whichever platform you used to purchase Daisy or meet me on my website, www.patbackley.com, to leave a review. I cannot wait to hear from you!

THANK YOU.

AUTHOR BIOGRAPHY

Pat Backley is an English woman who, at the age of 59, decided to become a Kiwi.

Now, she lives in New Zealand. When not writing, she loves to travel the world and particularly enjoys spending lots of time in Fiji with her beloved extended Fijian family or visiting her daughter, who currently lives in London.

She also gardens, paints, reads, and loves activities like interior design, walks on the beach, and socialising.

In short, she lives an ideal existence.

Not that it was always so easy, as her soon-to-be published memoirs will explain!

Made in the USA
Coppell, TX
01 December 2020

42677126R00141